Ravenwood:

A Seeker's Memoir

"In a small college town in the early Seventies three witches, a time traveler, a battle-scarred G.I., a French dress designer, a telepath and a chemistry student all walk into a bar...."

Through the years my life with the Garret Gang has often seemed like one of those jokes, though some of the humor has been very dark indeed. In our long journey toward the punch line we've seen worlds born and broken; gone skinny-dipping; lost love, and against all odds found it again; concocted potions; walked through fire; re-shingled a roof; fought elder horrors; played strip Tarot; wrestled with Death; laid some bricks; righted old wrongs; swapped war stories; had tea (well, cider, actually) with Gods and Guardians; befriended a lonely King; rescued a princess or two...

...And just incidentally, learned the Meaning of Life.

Ravenwood: A Seeker's Memoir is the tale of that journey.

Titles in the Ravenwood Series

Ravenwood: A Seeker's Memoir

The Moon Path (Book 1)

The Garret (Book 2)

The Magic Theater (Book 3)

Dark Domains (Book 4)

Out of Darkness (Book 5)

From Time Unforgotten (Book 6)

The Crypt (Book 7)

In Night's Labyrinth (Book 8)

Again to Live (Book 9)

The Dim City (Book 10)

Into the Depths (Book 11)

Second-Hand Gods (Book 12)

Syzygy! (Book 13)

Fools and Paladins (Book 14)

Moondark and Sunfire (Book 15)

Rain in the Garden (Book 16)

Fire and Water (Book 17)

The Book of Horab: A Ravenwood Tale

The Girl with No Name: A Ravenwood Tale

Grandmother Gingerbread: A Ravenwood Tale

The Book of Joys: A Ravenwood Guide

The Book of Silence: A Ravenwood Grimoire

Ravenwood:
A Seeker's Memoir

Book 1

The Moon Path
Jack Peredur

"...I shall not grow too old to see
Enormous night arise:
A cloud that is larger than the world
And a monster made of eyes."

-- G. K. Chesterton, "A Second Childhood" (1922)

www.Ravenwood.Associates

Ravenwood Associates, LLC
P. O. Box 916
Bath, SC 29816

Author's Disclaimer: This Memoir is my attempt to recreate events surrounding the 1972 Ravenwood disaster based upon my own memories, those of friends who lived through these events along with me, and documents we created at the time. As such it is necessarily, in part, a work of fiction. Many events described are reconstructions. For the sake of anonymity and privacy I have changed the names and some identifying details of all persons and locations, save for those few already well-known to the public through other accounts of the Ravenwood disaster. Any similarity of such names to those of actual persons or places is purely coincidental.

The Legal Disclaimer: This is a work of fiction. All the characters and events portrayed in this book are fictional, and any resemblance to real people and incidents is purely coincidental.

The Moon Path / Jack Peredur – 1st ed.

ISBN 9781086020182 (Paperback)

Dedication

I dedicate this work to the memory of the Ravenwood Thirteen, pioneers on the Moon Path; to all others who follow that path, whether only for a few steps or all the way to its unknown end; and especially to our friends and fellow travelers in Ravenwood Associates, a growing network created to honor their memory and carry on their legacy.

Are you already one of us, or would you like to be?

Find out more at
www.Ravenwood.Associates!

Preface

Those familiar with the history of America in the 1970s will recall the Ravenwood disaster, in which thirteen college students and faculty met their end in an apartment near Russell University in Columbia, South Carolina in the spring of 1972. Some truth, but much more falsehood, has been written about that incident. As a close friend of several of the deceased, it is my intent in this memoir to set the record straight.

While this account is as accurate as I have been able to make it -- based on my own memories, those of friends who lived through these events along with me, and documents we created at the time -- it still necessarily remains in part a work of fiction. Many events described, and nearly all dialogue, are reconstructions. Except for the names of those few persons already well-known to the public through other accounts of the Ravenwood disaster, all in this memoir, including brand names, are either fictitious or are used fictitiously. Similarly, locations not already well-known have been disguised by changing their names and other details.

The chemical steps I have described are mostly correct. Since my research at Calhoun University was never published, I include them hoping others may someday complete the work begun there. Sadly, since my notes were lost I have had to rely on memory and thus some errors may have crept in. To avoid loosing a potentially dangerous drug onto the streets, I have also left out or changed some crucial details. A legitimate researcher should be able to restore them, and correct any other mistakes, through literature review and a modest amount of experiment.

I broke no oaths of secrecy in the writing of this work. Where that would have occurred I have substituted new material, maintaining the spirit, flavor and function of the original. The same is true of material known or reasonably suspected to be under copyright, except for legal fair use or where express permission could be obtained.

On this, see the Acknowledgements page at www.Ravenwood.Associates for more information.

All else is truthful, to the best extent to which I now can make it. Believe of it what you will.

Jack Peredur
The Ravenstead
Lammas, 2019

"Magic's just somebody else's technology, that we don't happen to understand. Yet."

-- Nick Valentine's paraphrase of
Arthur C. Clarke's Third Law.

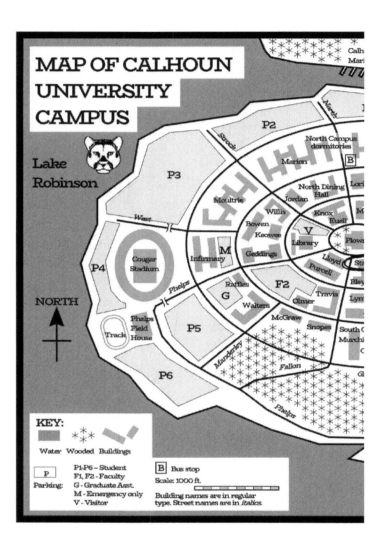

MAP OF CALHOUN UNIVERSITY CAMPUS

Lake Robinson

Calh...
Mari...

P2

North Campus dormitories

Strock

Marion

B

North Dining Hall

Lori...

P3

Moultrie

Jordan

North

Willis

Knox

M

Bowen

Euell

West

Keowee

V

Plow...

Library

Geddings

Lloyd

St...

M

Purcell

Infirmary

Bley...

Cougar Stadium

P4

Raffles

F2

Travis

Lyn...

Phelps

G

Olmer

Walters

McGraw

Snopes

NORTH

Phelps Field House

Track

P5

South C...
Murchi...
C...

Manderley

Fallon

G...

P6

Phelps

KEY:

Water   Wooded   Buildings

P — Parking:

P1–P6 – Student
F1, F2 – Faculty
G – Graduate Asst.
M – Emergency only
V – Visitor

B — Bus stop

Scale: 1000 ft.

Building names are in regular type. Street names are in *italics*.

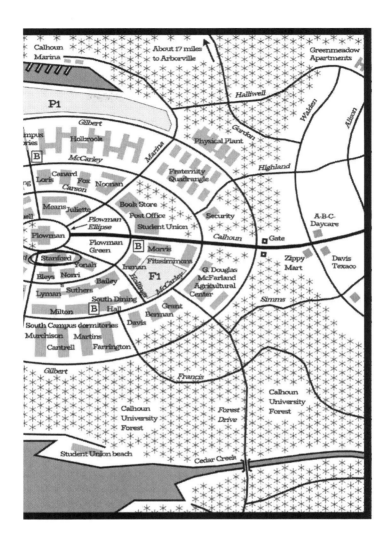

1971 Calendar

January

Sun	Mon	Tue	Wed	Thu	Fri	Sat
					1	2
3	4	5	6	7	8	9
10	11	12	13	14	15	16
17	18	19	20	21	22	23
24	25	26	27	28	29	30
31						

February

Sun	Mon	Tue	Wed	Thu	Fri	Sat
	1	2	3	4	5	6
7	8	9	10	11	12	13
14	15	16	17	18	19	20
21	22	23	24	25	26	27
28						

March

Sun	Mon	Tue	Wed	Thu	Fri	Sat
	1	2	3	4	5	6
7	8	9	10	11	12	13
14	15	16	17	18	19	20
21	22	23	24	25	26	27
28	29	30	31			

April

Sun	Mon	Tue	Wed	Thu	Fri	Sat
				1	2	3
4	5	6	7	8	9	10
11	12	13	14	15	16	17
18	19	20	21	22	23	24
25	26	27	28	29	30	

May

Sun	Mon	Tue	Wed	Thu	Fri	Sat
						1
2	3	4	5	6	7	8
9	10	11	12	13	14	15
16	17	18	19	20	21	22
23	24	25	26	27	28	29
30	31					

June

Sun	Mon	Tue	Wed	Thu	Fri	Sat
		1	2	3	4	5
6	7	8	9	10	11	12
13	14	15	16	17	18	19
20	21	22	23	24	25	26
27	28	29	30			

July

Sun	Mon	Tue	Wed	Thu	Fri	Sat
				1	2	3
4	5	6	7	8	9	10
11	12	13	14	15	16	17
18	19	20	21	22	23	24
25	26	27	28	29	30	31

August

Sun	Mon	Tue	Wed	Thu	Fri	Sat
1	2	3	4	5	6	7
8	9	10	11	12	13	14
15	16	17	18	19	20	21
22	23	24	25	26	27	28
29	30	31				

September

Sun	Mon	Tue	Wed	Thu	Fri	Sat
			1	2	3	4
5	6	7	8	9	10	11
12	13	14	15	16	17	18
19	20	21	22	23	24	25
26	27	28	29	30		

October

Sun	Mon	Tue	Wed	Thu	Fri	Sat
					1	2
3	4	5	6	7	8	9
10	11	12	13	14	15	16
17	18	19	20	21	22	23
24	25	26	27	28	29	30
31						

November

Sun	Mon	Tue	Wed	Thu	Fri	Sat
	1	2	3	4	5	6
7	8	9	10	11	12	13
14	15	16	17	18	19	20
21	22	23	24	25	26	27
28	29	30				

December

Sun	Mon	Tue	Wed	Thu	Fri	Sat
			1	2	3	4
5	6	7	8	9	10	11
12	13	14	15	16	17	18
19	20	21	22	23	24	25
26	27	28	29	30	31	

Table of Contents

1 Suzanne

May 15, 1971

Even after half a century I still wake sweat-bathed and shuddering from nightmare, ears ringing with the screams of friends far gone in agony and horror: wake but almost wish I hadn't, knowing they all might still be alive if I'd only stayed home in New Jersey.

But the dawn of the Seventies was a rough time for my family. The new chain stores were eating away at my Dad's hardware business, while year by year

Rutgers' tuition kept rising. By the middle of my senior year it was all too clear that while my grades would easily get me into graduate school, it would have to be somewhere cheaper.

My advisor suggested Calhoun University, in the inland corner of South Carolina. "The tuition, even out-of-state, is barely half what you'd pay here. But Calhoun has one of the best chemistry departments anywhere, and their graduate program's just been expanded. ...And I'm sure you've heard of Doctor David Knight?"

"From M.I.T.? The one who did so much pioneer work on nitrogen heterocycles?"

"The same. He's sent out a call for highly qualified students to come study there. And he's offering an assistantship with full tuition, plus a good stipend for living expenses, to whoever best qualifies."

"And you think I might?"

"You're at the top of your class in chemistry, and unless something goes badly wrong you'll graduate *cum laude*. I strongly urge you to write him and ask..."

So here I was, on a Saturday morning in the middle of May 1971: climbing the stairs in Stanford Hall, with copies of my Bachelor's diploma and Doctor Knight's acceptance letter neatly folded in my inside coat pocket. I'd reached the campus barely an hour before, after a sleepless redeye flight to Atlanta, a shuttle to the

Arborville airport, and a long bus ride from there. Parking my suitcases and battered old knapsack in a locker at the Student Union, I'd gotten a much-needed cup of coffee in the little canteen there and spent a few minutes at one of its tables studying again the map Doctor Knight had sent me.

After a short walk across the campus – nearly empty this morning, since the spring semester was over and the first summer session not yet begun – with the map's help I'd easily found Stanford Hall. The building too seemed almost deserted, but the door to room 227 stood open.

The occupant, deeply immersed in the contents of an open folder on his desk, didn't seem to notice me looking in. After a moment I knocked gently on the frame to get his attention. Looking up, he glanced from my face to an old wood-cased clock on the wall, then back to me, smiled, set the folder down on his desk, and stood. "Come in, come in." He spoke with a faint upper-class British accent. "You must be Jack Peredur: did I pronounce that right?"

"Close. It's 'PAIR-a-durr'."

Doctor Knight smiled. "And ten minutes early!"

He was formidable, this sage of chemistry: taller by several inches than my own five-ten, wearing glasses with thick black frames, and crowned by a mass of unruly white hair Albert Einstein might have envied.

We shook hands, and he showed me to a chair.

"You come highly recommended, Mr. Peredur." He got the pronunciation right this time. "Doctor Martinson sent me a copy of your senior report." One long finger tapped the folder on his desk, and I saw that its tab bore my name. "Very impressive. Is it true that you designed your own azepine synthesis?"

"Well, it was basically the method Paquette worked out at Ohio State. But I modified it a little…" and for half an hour or so we spoke the language of organic chemists, pausing now and again to sketch structural diagrams on notepad or blackboard.

Finally, Doctor Knight smiled. "I think that I was right to choose you. Do you know, there were almost fifty applicants? But I see you'll do nicely.

"Now here's what I want you to work on, this coming year." He placed in my hands the three-dimensional model of a complex molecule, variously-colored wooden "atoms" joined by short rods forming three interlocking rings. As I studied it, he sketched on a pad a flattened diagram of the same structure.

"This is 2,3,9-triazafluorene: a tricyclic system holding three nitrogen atoms, thus." He labeled them, then filled in numbers at the rest of the outer positions. "Some natural compounds, the harmala alkaloids, have the same structure with just two nitrogen atoms. But the three-nitrogen system doesn't occur in nature, and to my best knowledge it's never been made."

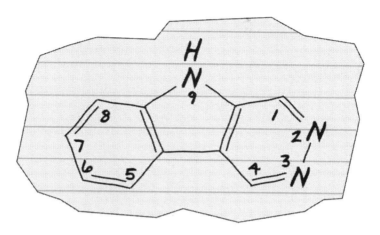

"And you want me to work out a synthesis?"

"Precisely. For the basic ring structure, and later for some of its simple derivatives. I want to contrast their properties with those of the already known compounds. I suggest you start your search with the review articles by Fisher and Wegener…"

Taking from the folder a list of journal articles he'd already compiled for me, he sent me off to look them up in the Research Library down the hall. I found it with ease; it was the last door on the right before the stairs at the end.

The room's center held old-fashioned, upright wooden bookcases full of chemical journals, textbooks, and other reference works. Along the walls, brown-tiled like those in the corridor and Doctor Knight's office, small tables and carrels had been set up for study. Choosing the nearest, I set his list down on its little desktop and went to look for the *Journal of Organic Chemistry.*

While searching the collection, though, I noticed a quiet sound coming from another carrel: the sound, I thought, of someone sobbing. Curious, I went on down the aisle to see what was wrong.

Her dark brown hair was gathered at the sides in loose pigtails, their canary-yellow bows matching her blouse. A purse lay open before her on the carrel's little desk, its contents dumped out and scattered – lipstick, a compact, loose change, a package of tissues – as if she'd been desperately searching through them for something lost. Two suitcases were on the floor beside her. And yes, she was crying.

"What's the matter? Can I help?"

She raised her head and looked at me, dabbing at her eyes with a crumpled tissue. They were as blue as a morning sky, though the lids were red and swollen....

And I recognized her. She'd been on the bus when I'd boarded it at the airport; she must have gotten off at the Student Union too.

"You are not Professor Blake, are you?" Through the tears in her voice, I could tell she had a strong accent. Was it French?

"No; sorry. I'm Jack Peredur: just a student, and new here myself."

She smiled, though sadly. "I am Suzanne Marat…and also new, as I am sure you can tell."

"Were you supposed to meet him here?"

"Yes, at ten-thirty. He was to help me register for summer classes and find a place to stay. But he has not come, and now it is past eleven! And somehow, I have lost the paper with his telephone and office numbers on it."

"Are you sure you're in the right place?"

"Yes, he was very clear. I was to wait for him in the Student Lounge, on the first floor of the chemistry building…"

"But this is the second floor: the Research Library!"

"No! I climbed only one flight of stairs. And this is the only room like a lounge which I could find."

"Wait a minute." My high-school French was badly rusty, long buried under the German all chemistry majors must learn, but I vaguely remembered… "If this is the 'first' floor, then what's the floor below us?"

"That is the…*rez-de-chaussée*…the ground floor. Why? Am I wrong?"

"A problem of idiom, I think. You're new in this country, aren't you?"

"Yes. I have been here only a few months, and I have still very much to learn. In America, is it called differently?"

"I'm afraid so. This is the second floor. The *rez-de-chaussée* – did I pronounce that right? – is what we call the first floor, here."

She looked up, now with the ghost of a smile. "Ah, yes: I had forgotten. This is still all so new to me, so many things to remember. Thank you!"

"No problem. So come on; let's see if we can find your Professor Blake."

While she returned the items to her purse I folded up Doctor Knight's list of journal references and put it in my pocket; I could look those up later. I picked up both her suitcases, and she followed me back down the stairs.

We found the Student Lounge with ease; it was directly below the Research Library. But Professor Blake wasn't there and hadn't left a note. Next to the soft-drink machine, though, was a pay phone, and below it hung two telephone directories: one for the campus, the other for the town of Calhoun beside it.

The campus directory listed three Blakes, but only one had an office in Stanford Hall: Room 134. So we went there and found him in: a small man with graying hair and gold-rimmed glasses, in a rumpled sport coat and no tie.

"Professor Blake? I am truly sorry that we missed each other. I am Suzanne Marat."

"Suzanne! What happened? I was afraid you'd had an accident or something, on the way down from Arborville!"

"I did, in a way. But this man rescued me…"

"Jack Peredur. It was nothing, really; just a difference of idiom…" and she and I, alternately, told the story.

"Good; no harm was done, apart from a little worry. And so: I understand you're new in town too?"

"As new as Suzanne. We came in on the same bus this morning. I'm from New Jersey."

"'Joisey'? I thought so, from your voice." He smiled. "So neither of you has a place to stay yet? Registration's still two days off, but there's no sense in your both having to sit in the gutter 'til then!"

"What did you have in mind?"

"Well, I once promised Clarisse Suzanne could stay with me, if she ever wanted to and I had room. I rent out my spare bedroom, but there've been no takers this summer. So, Suzanne, it's yours if you want it. And Jack…well, we'll work something out. Had you planned to stay in the dorms?"

"Yes. My dorm rent's already paid. Can't I move in yet?"

"Not until Registration. But since you rescued Suzanne, it's only fair I put you up on the couch until then. My house isn't far from campus, so I often go home for lunch and you're both welcome to come along. How do ham-and-cheese sandwiches sound?"

"Wonderful! I have not eaten since before the bus ride…"

Locking up the office behind us he left a note on the door, then led us outside and down the block to an ancient blue station wagon in the faculty parking lot. "Climb in!"

We swung past the Student Union, and I retrieved my luggage. Professor Blake talked constantly as he drove, and though Suzanne said little, I gathered that her Great-Aunt Clarisse had once taught at Calhoun and was an old friend of the professor, though she'd retired some years before.

Professor Blake – "Charlie," he corrected me when I called him that for the seventh or eighth time – lived alone in a small house about four blocks from campus, one in a line of a dozen or so which differed only in their colors. "When you're an M.S. in a Ph.D. world," he explained, "you don't get a mansion." But it was a comfortable little home, and the couch seemed quite adequate for two nights.

Suzanne, of course, had the back corner room to herself. It was not a large one, but there was a bed, and a small table which could serve as a desk, and a wheeled typist's chair pushed under it, and a dresser into which she immediately started unloading her suitcases.

That afternoon, after I'd caught some much-needed rest on that couch while Suzanne finished settling in, Charlie took us both on a walking tour of the campus. "This is Purcell Hall. Suzanne, as a liberal-arts major you'll probably spend most of your time here or in Travis across the street. ...And there's the Library. A lot bigger than the one in Stanford Hall, isn't it, Jack?"

Calhoun University is built on a hill, with Plowman Hall, the old administration building, at the top. Its distinctive clock tower, as much a school symbol as the Calhoun Cougar, is visible for miles. The other University buildings lie in descending tiers below it: academic buildings close in, then dormitories, with parking lots, the field house and the stadium forming an outer ring.

To the east is the town of Calhoun, covering the slopes of an adjacent hill crowned by the Cougar Hotel and a tall, silver-painted water tank. Descending through the tiers of the campus and the old brick gate at the bottom, Calhoun Avenue rises again becoming the town's main street, then continues through pine woods and farmland to meet State Highway 97 – "the Arborville Road" – in the little town of Seven Oaks a few miles further on. Our bus had come that way from the airport.

To the south lies an arm of Lake Robinson, a huge

artificial reservoir. Calhoun Hill – "College Hill," as most locals call it – forms a blunt peninsula jutting west into the lake, with Phelps Field House and Cougar Stadium near its tip. A lesser inlet to the north supports a small marina. Lake and town together nearly surround the campus, like mismatched parentheses.

I still had Doctor Knight's little map in my pocket, and marked our route lightly on it in pencil as we walked. By the end of the day, I felt I knew my way around campus fairly well.

But that knowledge had come at a price. My feet were sore from climbing up and down College Hill all afternoon, I was still short on sleep, and an old back injury, where I'd slipped a disk years before in my first and only game of tackle football, had started to throb dully but insistently. I was only too glad to ride back to Charlie's house, gulp some aspirin, and collapse back onto that welcoming couch.

Most of Sunday I stayed in the Research Library, poring over chemical formulae and synthetic procedures, and taking notes. A possible route of synthesis for making Doctor Knight's compound was taking shape in my mind, and I started drawing it out on paper, showing each needed structural change along with the chemical reagents which might bring it about.

Suzanne came up at seven to find me there, still working on it. "I thought that you might still be here.

Have you eaten?"

"I had lunch at the Student Union: a sandwich, coffee, and something called a Pluto Pie. Nothing since then. Why?"

"There is a restaurant near campus, the Cougar's Lair, which Charlie recommends. It is not expensive, and tonight it should not be crowded. I thought that if you wanted to, we could try it on the way back."

"Sounds good to me. Let me finish drawing this structure... And so the ring closes: a modified Bischler indole synthesis... There." I held it up. "How's that for a day's work?"

Her forehead wrinkled. "What is it? A new design for wallpaper?"

"It's what I'll be doing for the next year or so." And I tried to explain, as simply as I could, what the symbols meant...

Suzanne stopped me. "I have had very little chemistry: only the course at the *lycée* – the high school. I do not know what an indole is...although I do see, in your drawings, that the ring indeed closes."

"Now, if only it will in the lab! All this is tentative. There's no way to know if any step here will work or not, until I try it. But at least I have a rough plan to follow now." And gathering up the chemical journals I'd been using, I started carrying them back to the shelves where I'd found them.

"Let me help you with those." She bent to pick up one I hadn't been able to take on the first trip. "Jack? This book is in German!"

"Sure. Most of the chemical work before World War II was published in German." I explained about the foreign language requirement I'd had to satisfy at Rutgers. "And I understand they do the same thing here."

"But that is terrible: to have to learn a language, merely because of these old books! Why could they not pay someone to translate them for you?"

"Easier said than done, I'm afraid. This isn't just ordinary German; it's technical German, so the translator would have to be a chemist too. And chemists are paid to do chemistry, not spend a lot of time translating old journals.

"Besides, this stuff has been piling up for a century or more." I gestured around at the ranked journals, shelf on shelf, rack on rack. "Two or three million pages right here. And these are only the most popular journals, and a few reference works. The total literature could be ten times this much. And growing every month!"

"All of that, just for chemists?"

"Sure. 'Publish or perish'! Even Doctor Knight has to crank out at least a paper a year, or the Administration might start wondering why they're paying him so much. It's my job to help him."

As I shelved the last of the journals I carried, Suzanne held out the remaining three. "Are there then no French journals? Only German ones?"

"A few, but not many. A lot are in English now, and some in Russian, Japanese, Hindi…. Every language chemists speak, I guess. But that makes the problem even worse. Once you'd translated it all into English you'd have to do a French translation, and Russian, and Hindi… It's easier if we all just learn German, and translate bit by bit as we need it."

"Yes, I see that it is so. But still: could they not have chosen some easier language, in which to speak together? As once, all of the European royalty chose French?"

"The *lingua franca*? I wish they had. But it's about a hundred years too late to change it now!"

The sun was low in the sky behind us as we left the campus, following Calhoun Avenue as it dipped between the twin hills and then rose again to become the main street of the town.

The Cougar's Lair stood on a corner to our left, two blocks from the old campus gate; I recognized it now from the bus ride. The ground floor was obviously a beer parlor, the windows filled with those neon signs given away by the major brewers. The white wall above the entrance, bathed in floodlights, was painted with the huge, snarling head of a mountain lion, russet and black with eyes a fierce icy blue.

But Charlie had directed us to a more austere second entrance, on the side facing Alison Street. Stairs inside led up to a gallery, dimly lit and divided into booths, running around three sides of the huge room which seemed to fill most of the building. The center was open to the beer parlor below, reached by a spiral iron stair; the fourth wall was blank and white like a huge projection screen, visible from both levels of the... theater?

It puzzled my companion, too. "Jack, what is that?"

I saw a waitress approaching. "Let's ask... Do you show movies here?"

"You must be new at Calhoun. Did you come for the summer sessions?"

"Yes. We're both starting courses here."

"Well, the Lair's a local tradition." She jerked a thumb toward the row of framed posters mounted above the booths. "Friday and weekend evenings we have movies – classics and science fiction, mostly – or live entertainment. There's a stage below the screen, and in front there's a dance floor. If you lean over the rail, you'll be looking right down at them both.

"Tomorrow, from four to midnight, we're having a 'welcome back' special for the summer students...or 'welcome to Calhoun,' I guess, if you haven't been here before. Local bands, and a light show, and all the spaghetti or pizza you can eat for two bucks. And your second beer is half-price."

"Sounds good. Suzanne, do you like spaghetti?"

"Yes, of course! Shall we come?"

"Sure, I'd love to…"

Smiling, the waitress showed us to one of the booths and brought us menus: lists of pizza and pasta varieties, deli sandwiches, and an amazing selection of wines and beers. We decided to split an "Everything" pizza, hold the anchovies, and a carafe of Bordeaux Suzanne suggested would go well with it.

Halfway through the pizza, though, Suzanne looked past me with widening eyes. "Jack, you must see that!"

I turned so I could look over the booth wall behind me. The big screen was blank no longer; it writhed with moving colors, shapes which grew and broke apart, merged and shrank like globs of floating oil. As we watched, then, points of brighter light began to sweep up and down and sideways, appearing and disappearing, against the changing background.

The oil-shapes vanished, replaced by a moving lattice of geometric shapes which cycled individually through vivid colors, no two quite the same. And that, too, gave way to a succession of feathery, crystalline shapes in which the same pulsing colors streamed and pinwheeled.

The entire sequence could have lasted no more than five minutes. The flying light-spots faded out; then the crystal background dimmed and vanished as a deep voice came on the public-address system: "Just a sample, folks. Be here tomorrow night...and the Flying Fire will come, and take your mind a-waaay!"

I smiled in admiration. "Now, **that** was a light show!"

"I had never seen one before. How is it done? It is not a film, surely?"

"No. It's done with very specialized projectors, usually hand-built by the people putting on the show. There was a group back at Rutgers that did one; some of their members were in the Scarlet Players with me. But they were never as good as what we just saw!"

"This was very beautiful: very good, I suppose, though I know nothing of light shows. But we will see far more tomorrow night, will we not?"

"I'm planning on it. But I'll bet we could get a look at the equipment tonight, and meet the people behind it. The Rutgers group loved to show off their equipment...as long as nobody touched it!"

Visible beams of light during the show had revealed the booth's location: above and behind the restaurant booths, against the windowless patch of wall which, outside, bore the snarling cougar. After paying our check, we climbed the steps leading to it and found the door at the top ajar.

Only one man was in there: built tall and wide as any football player, with skin dark as baking chocolate, a full black beard, long kinky hair, and a black sleeveless shirt bearing some sort of neon-orange logo. His hands looked big enough to crush half-gallon cans. Anywhere else, I'm sure I'd have found him intimidating. Tonight, though, he was leaning close above a little workbench, wearing a magnifying visor and frowning in concentration while those huge hands manipulated tweezers and a tiny soldering iron, repairing an intricate printed-circuit board. The smell of melted flux filled the air.

We stood there in silence until he finished and looked up, setting the board down with a sigh. "Busted reed relay. Maybe it'll work now... Hi. I'm Nick Valentine. Of the Flying Fire."

"Jack Peredur, and Suzanne Marat." I took his offered hand and shook it. My own practically disappeared inside. "We loved the show, what there was of it. Better than any I saw back in New Jersey."

"Thanks. Sorry I didn't have everything working, but some of the equipment got shaken up on the way over here. This sound-sync, for instance..." and he gently tapped the board he'd been soldering. "I was just about to test the repair."

"Mind if we watch?"

"Not a bit. Let me put the board back in the cabinet..." and thrusting its edge firmly into a socket, he closed the cabinet lid and flipped a switch. "In fact, you can help if you like. Go out to that microphone – the one on the tripod, with the long tubes – and snap your fingers in front."

"Sure." I went back out and found the one he must have meant: a thing like a futuristic Gatling gun, a spiraling cone of metal tubes held together with plastic wire ties. At my finger-snap, brilliant light flashed from the booth.

"It works!" he shouted from within. "Thanks!"

I returned to see him tightening screws, sealing up the cabinet. "What is it?"

"Sound synchronizer: rigged up to trigger a strobe light on any loud noise. Tubes on the microphone make it directional. If a band were playing, I'd have it aimed at the drums.

"This little strobe..." and he patted the wooden case with its reflector and glass face... "is just for testing. Got two bigger ones out front, and they'd flash alternately: red on one beat, green on the next. But without the sound-sync, nothing worked."

He went on then to describe the other projectors he had with him, and show us what each one did: the turning, mirrored bowls which had made the moving dots of color, and the polarized-light wheels, and the other wheels of carefully crumpled metal which had helped form the shifting background shapes, and the ancient glass-slide projector, now heavily modified, which had made the patterns with the pulsing colors.

"Designed and built every one myself. And everything is controlled from this panel…"

"Do you mean you're the only operator? The group at Rutgers had five people in it, and they were all busy!"

"Trying to do it all by hand. No, I don't work that way. I **am** the Flying Fire, and I do it all. From right here!" and he caressed the control panel with its myriad of switches and dials and lights. "But I'm ready to shut it down 'til tomorrow. Why don't you come back then, and see it all in action? I'll be here five to midnight, running it whenever the bands are playing."

"Thanks. I think we will, at least for a while. That is, if Suzanne wants to."

"Of course I do! We will be here."

"Fine! I'll look for you." And he started throwing switches and turning knobs. The hum of cooling fans died. Lights began to wink out, and wheels fell still. The Flying Fire was extinguished…to be rekindled the following afternoon, at five.

Nick walked out to the curb with us. "I'd offer you a ride home…. Where is home, anyway, or are the dorms open now? …But I don't think you'd both fit."

"No; we would not." For his transportation was a huge black motorcycle, a Harley-Davidson scraped and dented from much hard use, parked in the alley behind the Lair. Its long narrow seat might have held someone behind him, but that single passenger would have had to be very small.

"Thanks anyway, though. We're staying with a friend until registration tomorrow. It's just a few blocks from here. We'll walk."

Welded just behind the seat was a large steel footlocker, closed by two padlocks. I tapped it curiously.

"That's the trunk: literally! All my projectors rode over in that."

"I can see why they got shaken up."

He nodded. "Had everything packed in foam rubber, but none inside the sound-sync box. Circuit board came unsocketed and banged around. Little glass relay got smashed. I'll know next time: pull that board out and stick it in my pocket!"

"Well, I hope everything works right tomorrow."

"Me, too...knock on chrome." He tapped the handlebar lightly with his knuckles. "See you then!" The motorcycle roared to life, and in thunder Nick vanished into the night.

So walking home, I had to tell Suzanne everything I knew about light shows. It wasn't much. "I had some free time my first year on Busch Campus, so I joined the Scarlet Players: sort of a stepchild of the Theater Department, meant for non-Theater majors. I did mostly lighting and special effects."

"'Special effects'? I am sorry; I do not know what that means."

"Rigging up gadgets, mostly. Our main play that year was 'Blithe Spirit,' about a man haunted by the ghost of his wife. The ghost moves things around, and throws things. So things on stage have to move, with nobody touching them. Only it was me."

"How?"

"With wires, mostly: fine steel wires the audience couldn't see. And about fifty little pulleys, bringing the ends together offstage so I could reach them all. Sort of like Nick's control panel."

"And did it work?"

"On dress-rehearsal night, one of the actors stumbled into my wires and tangled everything up. But the show ran five nights after that, and everything worked perfectly. Maybe because the director offered to make a ghost out of anybody who did that again, and let them do the moving and throwing!"

"To kill them? I hope that he was joking!"

"Mostly. But he was sure mad the night it happened. At me, first, until he realized what had happened!"

But she said nothing. In the light of the streetlamp,

her face showed grief. "Suzanne? What's the matter?"

"Jack, do you believe in ghosts? Real ones?"

"I don't know. Why?"

"Sometimes I think…"

"What?"

She shook her head. "Nothing."

"You can tell me. Did you see a ghost?"

Another head-shake.

"Then what is it?"

"Do not ask me that. It is…too painful."

"I'm sorry. Hey, can I help?"

"No. Just forget that I said it. Please."

"All right. But if I can ever do anything…"

"Thank you, Jack." She took my hand in both of hers. "I do not think so. Perhaps there is no one on Earth who can. But I will remember. Just in case."

We walked in silence after that, and when we got to Charlie's she went straight into her room and closed the door. I sat up for a while on the couch, reading over my notes from the day's work, and made a few additions to my master chart. When I looked at the clock again, it was close to eleven. Tomorrow would be Registration Day, and I'd need to be well-rested.

Shaking out the blanket Charlie had loaned me I spread it again over the couch, undressed, wrapped up in it, and slept.

2 Registration Day

May 17, 1971

Someone was shaking me. "Wake up, Jack. You will be late!" A woman's voice. With a French accent.

"Huh?" My dream was slow to fade. I'd been tangled in huge molecular models, and for a moment I'd thought her hand was an indole ring closing on my arm.

"It is seven-thirty already. We have to be at

registration in half an hour!"

Groggily sitting up, I realized the blanket was gone – kicked to the floor, no doubt in my dream struggles – and I was lying there in just my Jockey shorts. Embarrassed, I made a hasty grab for the blanket again and pulled it up over my lap.

Suzanne rolled her eyes, laughing. "Jack, I had four brothers in France. Should it bother me, to see you in…underpants?"

"I don't know. But I was an only child, and it does bother me a little. We hardly know each other!"

"Go, then, and dress yourself. I will turn my back. But hurry. We have so little time!"

So grabbing the clothes I'd worn the day before I ducked across the hall to the bathroom, washed and shaved as fast as I could, and dressed. Charlie had coffee ready in the kitchen, and I had just time to guzzle a cup before we left, chugging toward campus in his old blue station wagon. He parked in his assigned spot in the faculty lot, and Suzanne and I walked together up the hill to Plowman Hall.

We arrived there precisely as Registration opened at eight, but already the lines were long outside the doors. We spent nearly an hour standing in separate ones, "MNO" and "P-Z," waiting to get our registration packages. Finally reaching the head of the line, I received my little envelope of computer punchcards.

"Cards?" I'd asked Charlie the evening before.

He'd laughed apologetically, giving a little shrug. "I'm sure things are different at Rutgers now, but Calhoun still uses IBM cards. You'll need to walk them around campus and get them signed. Then they all go back to that mainframe in Plowman's basement to get read in...."

I found two seats side by side in the auditorium, waved to Suzanne, sat down, and opened the envelope.

It held four white cards, three more in assorted colors, a soft lead pencil, and an instruction sheet. The yellow card was Doctor Knight's guarantee of my tuition; the pink one acknowledged my dormitory rent was paid. The green asked if I wanted to buy a meal ticket...but Charlie had apologized for the food in the dining halls, too. Without hesitation I marked the "NO" block and thrust that card back into the envelope.

That left the white ones. The instructions showed what to do with them: fill out one for each course I wanted to take, then have it signed by the professor who'd be teaching it.

Suzanne joined me as I finished marking them, and I helped her fill out her own cards for the courses Charlie had suggested. We split up then, going in search of signatures: she to Purcell Hall, I to Stanford, agreeing to meet again in the Student Union for lunch.

Doctor Purvis signed my card without a second glance. Doctor Preston asked a few questions – had I taken analytical chemistry at Rutgers? What had it covered? How had I done? – but was easily satisfied, and signed too. Doctor Knight, though, wanted a full report on my research so far, and since I hadn't brought a copy of my master chart I had to try drawing it from memory. He made a few suggestions as I did, and gave me more references to look up. Overall, though, he was clearly pleased with the progress I'd made...and at last, he took my two remaining cards and signed them both.

Carrying my envelope back to Plowman Hall, I found the Bursar's Office and after another wait in line turned in all but the pink one. With that one stamped "MATRICULATION COMPLETE" I was off to the Dormitory Office, where after yet another wait I swapped it for two identical brass keys, "F-315" stamped on each. "Here's a map of the north campus dorms. This is Holbrook Hall; you can hardly miss it. 'F' wing is here. Go in the door at the near end, then up two flights..."

But it was already a quarter to one, so before looking at the room I went back to the Student Union and found Suzanne.

"Jack, I was beginning to think that you had fallen into chemicals and disappeared. I finished my registration nearly an hour ago!"

"I'm sorry. Doctor Knight wanted all the latest news. I guess he kept me most of that hour before he'd sign my cards. I still haven't seen the room they assigned me."

"Then after lunch we will get your luggage, and go up, and see it together."

"Fine. Shall we order? I'm starved!"

"Please, yes! I was going to wait just a few minutes more, then go and do it without you."

Getting hamburgers, fries and Cokes we took them back to a corner table, and while we ate, exchanged stories of our morning's adventures. "She almost would not sign my card for English 101; she said that my section was already full. But another was still open and did not conflict with my other courses. I will have to be there at eight o'clock instead of ten. But then I will have more time between classes, for studying!"

It was nearly three when we finally brought my suitcases back to campus and went in search of Holbrook Hall. It was, indeed, hard to miss: the first in a trio of serpentine masses of red brick and gray concrete, each four or five stories tall, winding for three long blocks along the northern slope of College Hill. The masonry was weather-stained, festooned with posters and handbills and the ragged taped corners left from others torn carelessly away. "Really looks like a slum, doesn't it?"

She nodded, face full of dismay. *"Un grand taudis!* And you have no choice but to live there?"

"Just for the summer. Maybe I can find a better place later on: some apartment off-campus, or a room like Charlie's... But why don't we see what it looks like on the inside?"

It looked like nothing so much as a prison. The interior walls were bare cinder block, painted a dull institutional green. Metal doors lined both sides, alternately brown and gray-blue, bearing tarnished brass numerals: E-128, E-129, E-130. The floor was tiled in vinyl, mostly gray but with obvious repairs in whatever colors must have been cheapest at the time. The ceiling was covered with fluffy, off-white stuff, likely asbestos, broken at intervals by heavy glass domes holding light bulbs, dust, and dead insects. The doors of a communal bathroom, now propped open, revealed a row of washbasins against a tiled wall. Many of the tiles were broken or missing.

Past the bathroom the corridor widened. To our left was a small study lounge open to the corridor, with tables, chairs and a row of vending machines. One table had already been claimed by students playing cards. A door beyond them opened to darkness; a sign above it read "STORAGE."

Opposite the lounge a stairway rose: iron steps and

iron-pipe rails, their paint chipped and scarred. I lugged the suitcases up two flights, wishing I'd brought less clothes on the plane; even wishing, toward the end of the climb, that I'd accepted Suzanne's offer to carry the smaller case for me. In my sedentary life this past couple of years, with little time for much but chemistry, I'd really gotten out of shape!

Above was a corridor just like the other save that its doors were numbered in the three-hundreds. To our right "F" section began: F-301, F-302, F-303. Reaching F-315 I pushed one of my new keys into the lock, turned it, and the gray-blue door opened before us.

It was a dismal little room, long and narrow, with only one window. On each side were a bed, a desk, and a tiny closet. Obviously I was to have a roommate again, as I had at Rutgers until my senior year. Remembering two of those roommates – the alcoholic and the playboy – I shuddered, wondering what sort of degenerate I might be forced to endure this summer.

There was already a clue, though. Folded sheets and blankets lay on one of the beds, and a suitcase stood, not yet unpacked, on the floor beside it. But a box of books on the desk stood open, and some were already arranged on the shelves above. "If he cares more about his books than his clothes, he can't be too bad."

"Yes, Jack. But look at the books which he has

brought. What a strange mixture!"

They were mostly physics textbooks: enough to show my roommate was clearly majoring in that subject, and by now either a senior or a graduate student like myself. Others were fantasy or science fiction: *Dune, Dangerous Visions, Stranger in a Strange Land,* Tallwin's Midrealm trilogy, and some others I didn't recognize.

There was a dictionary, of course, and a thesaurus, and a Bible, and a copy of the *Handbook of Chemistry and Physics*, identical with the one I'd bought in my junior year at Rutgers. But among these were titles I'd never have expected to find on a physics major's shelves. *Man and His Symbols. Altered States of Consciousness. Hypnotism: Its Power and Practice.* And one black paperback titled, in red letters, *Mastering Witchcraft.*

Curious, I started to pull that last one from the shelf. Just then, though, I heard another key in the lock, and the door opened. A short, red-haired young man came in, panting and staggering under the weight of a second big cardboard box…which I saw, when he put it down, was also full of books. "Hey there." He sat down on the bed, breathing hard. "Hadrian Marsan. And you?"

I introduced myself. "You must be a physics major."

"Yep. Finishing my B.S. this summer. What are you

in?"

"Chemistry. Just starting on my Master's. And Suzanne's a new freshman, in Liberal Arts. She'll be staying off-campus."

"Lucky lady. This place is really a dump, isn't it?"

"Yeah. It reminds me of a prison."

"It'll be better once we redecorate. I've got two more boxes to bring up..." and he heaved himself back up off the bed. "Mostly the stuff I had in Marion Hall, before they closed it for the summer to put up more of this ceiling fuzz." He jerked a thumb up at our own ceiling, his distaste clear. "I had that room fixed up right!"

"Can we help?"

"Nope. None of the rest is heavy. I've got all my books here now."

"We were looking at those. You've got some unusual titles."

"The parapsychology ones?"

"If that's what you call it. Hypnotism and witchcraft?"

"Those are just two more roads leading to the same place. Everything's connected, down on the quantum scale. The challenge is to figure out how!"

"You mean you believe in that stuff? A physics major?"

"Why not? Telepathy exists; Rhine proved it back

in the Fifties. It's still not in most of the books, but it's real, all right. Explain how it works, and you'll understand how a lot of other things fit together too."

"Well, maybe. Rhine hasn't proven it to me, yet!"

"You haven't read his books. Be my guest!" and he waved at the shelf. "I'll be back later. But I have to get those other boxes out of the storeroom now, before somebody else does."

Without further ceremony, he turned and left us. There was something odd in the way he walked, even without books to carry…but before I could quite figure out what it was, the door was closing behind him.

Suzanne shook her head. "What a strange little person!"

"Yeah. But at least he's not a drunk like my sophomore-year roommate. Physics isn't an easy course. So if he's made it this far, I doubt he spends much time partying."

"And, in any case, it is only for the summer. Then he will leave…"

"And the Dorm Office will put in somebody worse, and I'll still be stuck in this little room. No, I think I'll keep my eyes open for a place off-campus!"

"Jack, it is already four o'clock. Nick is expecting us at the Cougar's Lair at five, is he not?"

"Or whenever we get there. I'd like to unpack a little, though. It'll probably be late when I get back, and tomorrow's a class day."

"Certainly. Can I help?"

"You can help me make up the bed. Here, let's unfold this sheet…"

Five o'clock saw the bed made up, my clothes put away, and the few books I'd brought arranged on the shelf over my own desk. Hadrian hadn't yet come back. "Perhaps he decided that it was too much work and went to the Lair instead…

"Jack, I am hungry. How about spaghetti?"

"Sounds good to me." So we left the room, and I locked it again.

Holbrook Hall was gradually coming alive. More doors were open now, and people were coming and going in the hallways. Somewhere a radio was playing. The air already carried a taint of cigarette smoke. It was beginning to sound and smell like a dormitory.

But it still looked like a prison. And I doubted there was much either Hadrian Marsan or I, through chemistry, physics or witchcraft, would be able to do about it.

3 Alaine

May 17, 1971

It was about five-thirty when we got back to the Cougar's Lair. The beer hall was packed, the door wide open, a crowd gathered outside. Giving that a wide berth, we went around to the side door.

But we'd been standing there only a few minutes when our waitress from the night before came up to us, referred to a slip of paper in her hand, and asked, "Jack

...**Parader**? And Suzanne Marat?"

I smiled at her mispronunciation; it was far from the first time I'd heard it. " 'PAIR-a-durr.' Yeah, that's us!"

"Nick Valentine asked me to watch for you, and bring you to the projection booth when you came."

"Great!" So we followed, running a gauntlet of dirty looks from the rest of the line.

The fire was flying already. A band was playing down on the stage, bathed by the alternate flashes of red and green strobes. The big screen was full of colors. Flowing shapes slithered through geometric lattices, with darting bright spots flashing over all.

"Jack! Suzanne! Come on in!"

Nick's booth hummed and whirled and sparkled. Every piece of equipment he had was doing something...yet Nick, himself, seemed to be doing nothing but glancing occasionally out at the screen and adjusting controls on his panel. A girl was with him, gathering up strange oversized cards from a table bearing the wreckage of a pizza. We seemed to have come in just at the end of some sort of game.

"Hello, Nick. Thanks for sending for us. We could have been in that line for another half an hour! Who's your friend?"

"Meet Alaine Lancaster. Calhoun's resident *Romni* lady...."

"Resident what?"

She smiled. "What used to be called a Gypsy. Some consider that an insult, though. So out of respect, I've asked Nick to call me a *Romni* instead."

"...And Alaine, these are Suzanne Marat and Jack Peredur. They helped me fix the strobes last night."

"Not at all! We came up just as he finished."

"Well, Jack helped me test the repair. And it worked! So maybe Suzanne brought me luck."

Alaine – "with an 'A,' not an 'E'!" – wore many rings, but otherwise didn't look like a classic Gypsy to me. She was olive-skinned, yes, but her eyes were a very light brown, almost golden. Her hair, worn long and slightly curled, nearly matched them.

"Why does Nick call you a Gyp.... Sorry. A *Romni*?"

"Because..." her voice grew quiet... "I can see the future!" Then she smiled. "Sometimes."

"What do you mean?"

"I read the cards. It's just a hobby, but sometimes it seems to work." She tapped the cards in her hand. "I was just doing it for Nick."

"Fortune-telling cards?" I bent to look at those left on the table. They bore pictures, colored line drawings a bit like those in a comic book: dogs howling at the moon, a tower hit by lightning, a woman with a lion, people holding cups or swords. First my roommate, now this engineer? "Nick, you believe in this? As much as you're into high technology?"

His grin held no embarrassment. "Yeah. Seen it work too many times not to. It's like Clarke said at that sci-fi convention a year or two back: 'Magic is just somebody else's technology, that we don't happen to understand. Yet!' Or something like that."

"Well, I guess seeing's believing. I'm a skeptic, though, 'til I've seen for myself. So, show me. How do they work?"

Alaine smiled. "Each one has a meaning. Some people use regular playing cards, but I prefer these. The person who wants the reading shuffles them; then I lay them out in a pattern and read them…. Nick, may I explain this reading? Just the basics."

"Go ahead."

She began laying back down the cards she'd been gathering, restoring the pattern they must have formed. "Nick moved here about six months ago, from Arizona. There was a girl there named Dawn who'd meant to come with him…."

"My artist friend. She designed my Flying Fire logo," and he tapped the front of his shirt, turning to show it better: twin flaming "F's" entwined and flanked by fiery wings. "Had to stay put a while longer, though. So I asked the cards, would she be coming soon?"

"And they said…?"

Alaine laid a final card back in place. "We'll take them in order, starting with the pair in the center. Those represent forces within the person the reading concerns, In this case, that's Dawn. Traditionally they're read as two opposite forces, like 'greatest hopes' and 'greatest fears'.

"The Six of Cups, and the Four of Swords. Remembering happy times with a loved one. But fearing that person may now be lost forever."

"Well, that fits pretty well!"

"The four around them are outside influences." She laid a hand lightly on each in turn. "The Nine of Cups: material wellbeing. The Four of Cups: discontent even in the midst of that; something vital is still missing. The Falling Tower: breaking existing patterns, making room for the new. And the Moon: a journey ahead, to a goal still unknown.

"Then the vertical row: a chronological series. The past is the Seven of Pentacles: slow progress through many delays. The present, though, is Strength: the woman taming the lion. It says love can triumph over all that."

I was one card behind. "The Seven of what?"

"Pentacles. The disks there: each has a five-pointed star on it, a pentacle. In a common deck, I think they'd be the diamonds."

She tapped the next card, on which a mounted knight carried another of the starry disks. "The near future is the Dark Knight, the Knight of Pentacles: the one card in all the deck most nearly representing Nick himself. We call that his significator. It comes up in most of his readings.

"And the more distant future, the final outcome: Temperance." The card showed an angel pouring water or wine from one chalice into another. "No, not abstaining from alcohol. More like 'tempering' hot steel in cold water. It's the combination of two different things – the contents of the chalices – making a single, greater thing. Here, I think, two personalities…"

"Nick and Dawn?"

She nodded. "As I see it, then, Dawn is on the point of leaving right now: dissatisfied with where she is, and about to change her lifestyle, to set out on a journey. Where? To the Dark Knight; to Nick. And with what result? Temperance: the union of opposites."

"Then how long will it take?"

She shook her head. "The cards don't say that: only that it **will be.** But we've taken these readings before, and this is the first time a Major Arcanum has ever fallen in the 'present' position. Always before it's been a minor card of indecision, stagnation. And because of that, I'd say Dawn should be on the road within a month...and here, I'd guess, by the summer's end."

"What's a Major Arcanum?"

"One of the twenty-two cards that don't belong to any suit. Some consider them a suit in their own right: the suit of Trumps.

"A regular card deck has four suits: hearts, spades, clubs, and diamonds. The Tarot has cups, swords, wands, and pentacles. Those represent forces coming from other people, or from things on the Earthly plane. But the Tarot adds that Trump suit, for spiritual forces: guidance from beyond this world."

"From the Moon?" I tapped that card.

"Not literally. There's also a card for the Sun, and one for a Star, traditionally Sirius. But they're all symbolic. The Sun represents healing and renewal, and the Star, 'don't give up hope'!"

I was intrigued. First Hadrian and his faith in telepathy, now this? I'd come a long way from Rutgers! "I'm still not sure I believe in it...but could you do a reading for me? To tell how I'll do here at Calhoun?"

"Sure. Not tonight, though. If I do two in a row, the second one never seems to work. But I live in the dorm: Farrington Hall, on the south side of campus. Room 405. Maybe some night, both of you can come up...and you too, Nick! We can make it a foursome."

"And we will bring the wine! …Alaine, I must confess: when first you began to talk about fortune-telling, I was frightened. Always, I was taught that such powers are from the Devil. But there is no evil in it, is there? It is more like putting together a jigsaw puzzle! So perhaps, another night, you can do it also for me?"

"Of course, Suzanne. But now that I think of it, there's one thing we can probably still do tonight if you like. The simplest of all Tarot readings: to tell what the coming year will bring."

She pushed the cards together, brought the rest of the deck from a pile at the back of the bench, and shuffled them all together. "There, that should be enough." Then, fanning them and holding them out face-down: "So, pick a card. Any card."

"But I cannot see them. How should I choose?"

"Close your eyes. Move your hand back and forth, and take whichever one just somehow feels right."

Suzanne did so, finally picking one from near the left edge of the fan. "Should I show it to you?"

"Not yet. Now you, Jack."

I closed my eyes and reached out. My fingers started to close on a card…and something within me wordlessly advised *The next one*. So I moved one card to the right, drew it out, and looked.

It was the Moon.

"All right. Suzanne, what's yours?"

"Three…the Three of Cups. Is it a party?" She held it up for us.

Three people in a garden raised cups as if toasting each other. Two were clearly women. We saw only the back of the third, who, though long-haired, might have been of either sex.

"It could be a party. It usually means new friendships, or sometimes a joyful reunion with old loved ones."

Suzanne smiled. "Already I am making new friends: Jack, and the two of you…"

"See? The cards don't lie! Though sometimes we can misread them… Jack, what's yours?"

"While you three are having your party, I'm supposed to go take a long walk. In the dark." I displayed the Moon card: a road emerging from water in the foreground and winding away into mountains, flanked by grim stone towers under a skull-like moon. Dogs, or perhaps a dog and a wolf, howled by the water's edge.

Reaching out Alaine gently took the card and gazed intently at the image on it. "A Major Arcanum guides you…" she murmured, then for long seconds was silent. When she continued it was more slowly, her voice very solemn.

"Jack, this will be a year of growth for you: learning new ideas, and stretching your mind to the utmost. And it won't always be in familiar, or even comfortable ways. You've learned a lot in the material world. Now you need to extend that into realms of imagination and intuition.

"It won't be an easy journey, nor always a safe one. The path is steep sometimes, and dangers lurk in the shadows. But the light of the Moon is there to guide you...and others have passed that way before. Heed well the signs they've left!"

She took a deep breath, blinked several times, then

reached for a napkin to blot a forehead suddenly beaded with sweat. "Wow! Where did all **that** come from?"

"Your *Romni* blood at work, Alaine."

"But I don't have any *Romni* blood, Nick. Not really…"

"Got it from Aunt Theda's cooking, then."

"Maybe. But Nick, I could actually see Jack walking away down the Moon Path. Not just in the picture, but as if that were a real place." She smiled, eyes wide with wonder. "In all the years I've been reading the cards, that's never happened before!"

"Shouldn't it, though? Isn't that what real fortune-telling is all about?"

"I guess so."

"Then, before it fades, tell us everything you remember." He searched the bench, found a pencil and a scrap of cardboard. "I'll write it down."

"It was as if a mist came over the card, and then spread over everything else. And then it cleared, and I was standing on a hillside, at night. I could feel the chill of the night air. There was a long road winding away, just as on the card…and beyond it the towers, and the Moon.

"I didn't see the dog and the wolf, or the water at the bottom. Just the road, gleaming like gold from the Moon's reflection, and Jack walking away, further and further. Then it all faded, and it was just a card again.

"Nick, I think I've had my first real 'psychic flash'!"

He was still writing. "Sounds that way. Maybe you've just learned to use the Tarot like it was meant to be used!"

"Maybe, finally, I'm learning to use my mind like it was meant to be used."

"'Opening your third eye', you mean?"

She grimaced. "What a horrible phrase! You've been reading that Tibetan stuff again. But yes: opening the mind's eye to see what is, and what will be. Now, if I can only learn to do it consistently..."

"Then you can hang out your shingle: 'Lady Alaine, Professional Psychic'!"

This time it was a glare. "You know we're forbidden to take money for the Art! It's the Law..." and then she broke off abruptly, looking at Suzanne and me as if to see whether, possibly, we might not have noticed what she'd said.

"The Law?"

"Ah... Aunt Theda lived with Gypsies for a while, years ago. A rather special group of Gypsies. They taught her some of their secrets, and she taught me. But along with the teaching comes the Law: never use it to hurt anyone, and never put a price on it."

"But I've seen Gypsies' signs along the highway:

'Mother Mary, Healer and Advisor'. There's one in Seven Oaks; we passed it coming here from the airport. Are you telling me Mother Mary does it for free?"

"No, of course not. There are Gypsies and Gypsies. Some know more than others. I'm sure some are just skilled guessers. Some probably aren't *Romni* any more than I am. But Aunt Theda's were…different. Some of them could do…well, what I did tonight, I guess. But better, and whenever they wanted to."

"Interesting people!"

"To put it mildly." She cocked her head. "Nick, the band has finished. Kill your lights!"

Big hands reached out and pulled switches. The spinning and sparkling stopped; only a soft whir of cooling fans continued. "You two ought to get some spaghetti; it's the special tonight. Could use some more myself, too. How about you, 'Lady Alaine'?"

"No, thanks. I'm stuffed! But go ahead; I'll watch."

He leaned out the door of the booth, waved, and soon our waitress came. "How are you doing? Need something else?"

"One refill and two starters. Another Michelob… and what for you two?"

"I do not like beer. Water only, for now."

"Make mine a Budweiser."

"I need your plate."

"Oh. Sorry." Nick handed it to her.

"And I'll take that one too, if you're done with it…"

Alaine passed hers over, and the waitress took them away.

"Where were we, now? Oh, yes: the Gypsies."

"Right. My Aunt Theda lived a while in England, back before World War Two; that's a long story in itself. But while she was there, she met these Gypsies and gradually made friends with them. They're a secretive people, and it took her years to gain their trust. But finally they took her in…and since they could see she had some natural talent, they taught her.

"Years later she came back to this country, to a farm in the Georgia hills my grandmother had left her. Then, when I was twelve, my parents died in a car crash. She was my only living relative, so I went to stay there with her.

"She was old then, well past eighty, but still spry as any twenty-year-old: from drinking herb teas, she said, and keeping active. She spent most of the day working outdoors, and she had the most wonderful garden I've ever seen. I think her thumbs must have been green clear up to the elbows! And she taught me, too: plant lore, and a lot of what she'd learned in England, including the Law and how important it was to keep it.

"And then, a month before my high-school graduation, I came home and found her dead. Still sitting up in her favorite chair." Her voice was getting ragged. "With one of her herbal books open in front of her. It was a stroke, the doctor said: sudden, massive, and fatal.

"She'd left me everything: the farm, and a little money, and…some other things. I finished out the school year somehow. Then I sold the farm, and put the money in a bank, and came here: to major in horticulture, and maybe use some of her knowledge to make the world a better place. That was three years ago. And that's the story of my life."

"Left out something, didn't you?" He gave her a sloppy military salute.

"Oh, Carl! No, we mustn't forget Carl!"

"In the military?"

She nodded. "In the Army. In Viet Nam."

"Oh, no!"

"I met him my sophomore year. We had Fall Semester together, and it was perfect. But then he ran out of money, and wouldn't let me help support him. Come Spring he dropped out to find a job. But one found him instead. 'Greetings'!"

I winced, remembering how narrowly I'd dodged that same barely-metaphorical bullet. "How much longer does he have to serve?"

"Until next April first. Ten more months. Three hundred and…eighteen days."

"April first? April Fools' Day?"

"That's the day they told him to report for duty. He joked about it: said it must mean he wouldn't have to serve the full two years. But they haven't let him out yet..."

"*Rom*-lady and I have something in common. Somebody else, a long way off!"

"Have you done card readings for Carl, too?"

"So many I've lost count! But I guess he's too close to me. When you try reading for yourself, or someone very close, the cards just repeat things you already know. At least, they do for me."

"Maybe that's why it took Jack to 'open your third eye.' Somebody you barely knew."

"Could be. I don't often read for people I've just met, or even mention the cards. Too many would treat it as a joke, or worse. Welcome to the Bible Belt! But when Nick said you two were coming, since I already had them with me, I drew one to see what our relationship would be in the coming year.

"I didn't get a psychic flash from it..." she riffled through the cards... "but it was a Major Arcanum. One of the best! ...Ah, here it is. The Hermit."

A bearded figure, cloaked in gray and leaning on a staff, stood looking down from a mountain peak at night. One hand held up a lantern, as if to illuminate the scene below or guide someone traveling there. "What does it mean?"

"A guide on your journey. A guide on the Moon Path."

"Well, Alaine, *Romni* Hermit, we welcome you. Guide ahead!"

"I wish it were that simple. I'm not much of a guide. I'm not standing on the peak, just finding my own way along the road, and I'm afraid my lamp isn't much. But maybe I can add a little light to the Moon's. And maybe you can help guide me, too…"

Our waitress reappeared, tray in hand, and suddenly it was spaghetti time. Suzanne and I found ourselves ravenous, and for a time we ate almost without words. But finally our appetite slackened, and Alaine picked up the conversation again.

"Now you know all about me. So, tell me about yourselves."

"For me, there's not a lot to tell. I'm from New Jersey, a place called Mount Laurel: a suburb of Camden, across the river from Philadelphia. My father runs a hardware store, and I've worked there part-time most of my life. Stocking shelves; helping customers; doing home repairs and installations."

"And when you're not doing that?"

"I've always loved science, especially the hands-on kind: experiments I could do myself. My last year in high school, my project won the school science fair and took third place in the regional. 'Amino Acids in

Common Proteins.' Doing it really sparked my interest in chemistry, so at Rutgers I decided to major in it.

"I got my B.S. there: my first year in Camden, the rest at Busch Campus in New Brunswick. Then I won an assistantship to come here for my Master's…and here I am. I start class tomorrow."

"Hobbies? Outside interests?"

"I read a lot: science fiction, mostly. And I used to collect rocks, back when I had the time. The old mine dumps at Franklin still have great minerals, and summers I'd fit in a collecting trip or two. I learned to cut and polish some of what I found, and do some metalwork too, making settings for them. But all my rocks and equipment are back in Mount Laurel, in storage. Too heavy to bring down."

"Too bad. Suzanne, how about you?"

"I am from Mortagne-au-Perche: a small town in Normandy, south of Le Havre. I was the oldest child of seven. Our father was a cabinetmaker. There was never enough money, so one of my chores was to make the clothes for us all, and keep them in repair. So after the *lycée* – here, you would call it high school – I left home, and went to Paris, and found a job in a dressmaker's shop.

"Then…then I decided to leave France, and came here instead: to join my Great-Aunt Clarisse, who had married an American but is now a widow. She has

Jack Peredur

The Moon Path

given me the money to come to college…and like Jack, I will start classes tomorrow."

"Why did you leave France?"

"I…." Suzanne shook her head. "I am sorry. I do not like to talk about it."

"That's O.K. Didn't mean to pry."

"And what are my interests? I enjoy cooking, and eating what I cook. I like to take long walks in the country when the weather is pleasant. East of Mortagne there are hills, and I would walk among them for hours. I like to swim, though I have had little chance since the…since I left Paris. And when I must stay inside I like to design clothes, or to make them."

"Did you make these?"

"Yes. The blouse is of my own design. The skirt I made also, like those which I wore at home. I am not yet comfortable in skirts so short as many wear them here. Not in public!"

"Neither am I. That's why I wear jeans."

"I have never worn trousers. Do you not feel strange in men's clothes?"

"It's no big thing. Whatever feels comfortable, that's what you should wear. As long as it doesn't get you arrested!"

"Yes, I suppose that it does not really matter. But this is what is most comfortable for me!"

And then the public-address system came on again,

Jack Peredur   55

announcing the next band to play.

Nick rose, lifted the tray from the old glass-slide projector, and replaced it with a new one. Walking once around the booth he changed out a wheel here, a color filter there, then sat again where he'd been when we'd arrived and began throwing switches and turning knobs on his main panel. "Setting up some different effects this time, since it's a different band!"

The band was different: that much, at least, could be said for them. They called themselves the Moody Funks, and they were terrible. The electric guitars sounded like tortured cats, while the drummer, I thought, would have been better employed splitting rocks on a chain gang. Maybe they'd written all their own songs, or maybe they were playing old favorites so badly we couldn't recognize them. In either case, I felt sorry for anyone near the speakers. The music was almost painfully loud even up here in the booth.

Still, Nick's strobe responded perfectly to that over-zealous drummer, and his colored lights turned the four sequined costumes into blazes of many-hued glory. If only we'd all been stone deaf, the Moody Funks might actually have been enjoyable.

"...So what about you?" I asked Nick, when once again we could converse without shouting. "You know my story, and Suzanne's. What's your background?"

"I'm a local boy..."

The Moon Path

"I thought Alaine said you'd come from Arizona?"

"I'll get to that. Grew up in a little place called Belvedere, just across the state line from Augusta, Georgia. Started here in '67, in double-E: electrical engineering…" he waved toward the spin and glitter… "as if you couldn't tell!

"Got involved with some off-campus bikers, though, and then drugs. Flunked out midway of my junior year.

"University has a policy for that, a one-time good deal: expunged my 'F's,' gave me a year's suspension, and said I could register again at the end and repeat the courses I'd failed. Decided to see the world a little in the meantime, and talked three other bikers into going with me. Saw quite a bit of it: Atlanta, New Orleans, San Antonio, Phoenix…

"Met Dawn in New Orleans; she was a runaway too. Sort of adopted each other. She reads the stars the way Alaine does cards. Did both our charts, and they fit together just like our personalities. Rode the back of my bike clear to L.A., and stayed for three of the wildest months ever. Parties and dope every night!

"It was too much. We both got tired of it and decided to leave. But on the way back, near Phoenix, the bike died. Hitched a ride into town in the back of a pickup truck, with five dollars and thirty cents between us. Got a job in a radio repair shop; Dawn went to work

Jack Peredur

57

as a waitress.

"Things went fine through the fall. Got the bike fixed but we decided to stay put, keep working and save our money so we could get back here without any more trouble. But then Dawn started to change."

"Change? How?"

"Having awful nightmares, and brooding a lot, and flaring up at me for no reason. Thought she was having a nervous breakdown, but one night she got out her charts and swore she'd spotted the problem. Uranus was transiting her natal Venus-Saturn conjunction..."

"Sorry, Nick. We don't know what that means."

"Guess I've heard her talk about it so much, I just assume everybody knows."

He raised a closed fist, palm toward us. "When she was born, Venus and Saturn were 'conjunct' – that means sitting in the same spot in the Zodiac – and dead overhead." His index and middle fingers rose side by side to point upward. "Mars and Neptune up close by, too. Uranus was ninety degrees off: in 'square,' as they say. Ascendant's the point just crossing the horizon, so that was ninety degrees off the other side..." His thumb and little finger folded out, making an inverted "T" in the air, leaving his ring finger still pointing down across his palm. He wiggled it for emphasis, "With Jupiter straight down below all the rest.

"Astrologers call that a 'Grand Cross.' Nasty! All

the negative aspects reinforce each other. And even worse for Dawn, since the top held two planets instead of one." This time it was the index and middle fingers that wiggled. "Called that spot 'the scar in her sky.' Blamed it for bad health when she was a kid and trouble with her father, a real horror show of a childhood.

"Last November, Uranus had moved through the sky just those ninety degrees…and it rubbed across the scar: rubbed it raw." His thumb came up to scrape across the fingers beside it. "Uranus brings instability and sudden change. For Dawn, it was pretty bad."

"But that was November. Why hasn't she come yet?"

"Uranus rubs the scar three separate times: last November, last April, and again next August. See, Uranus goes so slowly the Earth passes it and makes it seem to back up a while. Zig-zags across the sky like an eraser: back and forth, back and forth…." He illustrated, moving his thumb.

"During each pass she'd be shaken up, riding her emotions like a surfer on a bad wave. Not a good companion for somebody starting school again, and she knew it. So she wouldn't come. Decided to stay in Phoenix, since it was familiar by then. Hoped it'd give her a little stability.

"What she was really dreading, I think, was the

retrograde pass: the April back-swing. Usually brings some pretty drastic changes. That's the one that just ended. But from Alaine's reading, it sounds like she came through it all right."

"Why didn't you stay with her?"

"Wouldn't let me. Practically ran me off, finally. Said if I didn't come back and go to school when I was supposed to, she'd leave herself. Promised to come join me here, though, if she could, when it was over. I've rented a trailer so we'll have a place.

"Alaine's cards say she came through the retro-pass pretty well, and she's ready now to travel. And when Uranus makes the final, forward pass, at least we'll be together."

"Nick, you haven't got some extra room in that trailer, have you?"

"Not if Dawn's coming. Why?"

"I'll be looking for a place to stay off-campus, come fall. Maybe even sooner. I just checked into Holbrook Hall, and it's really a dump!"

He nodded. "Spent two and a half years there myself. Another reason I went looking for the trailer."

"Well, if you hear of anybody with a back room for rent, or an apartment that's not too expensive, would you let me know? I don't want to spend the next two years cooped up with some nut job in a little green prison cell!"

"Sure. Alaine, do you know of anything?"

"No, but I'll keep my ears open. Suzanne, where are you staying?"

"With Professor Blake, of the Chemistry Department. He is an old friend of my Great-Aunt Clarisse, and he has a vacant room now that his daughter is married. But there is only the one room…" and she explained how until this morning I'd been sleeping on his couch.

Alaine laughed. "No, that won't do. And I guess he'd be shocked if you both moved into that room…"

"He is not the only one who would be shocked!"

"Okay. Jack, if I hear of anything you'll be the first to know."

Our waitress came back then, and at Suzanne's suggestion we ordered a bottle of wine: the same imported Bordeaux we'd had the night before with our pizza. Over it, the four of us compared notes on life at Calhoun: where to eat, where to buy socks and underwear and toothpaste, when the campus bookstore might be least crowded, and which foods in the dining halls – should we be forced to eat there – were the most palatable, or at least the safest.

At nine the music started again: mid-Sixties muscle-car songs, from a five-piece group called "Grease Gun." They weren't as bad as the Moody Funks, nor, mercifully, quite as loud. Nick's lighting helped, but I guess the audience just wasn't nostalgic for "Little Cobra" and "409." There was little applause, and after those songs and a couple more the band packed up and went away again.

"Nick, Alaine, we really ought to go. We both have eight-o'clock classes tomorrow."

"You know, the first band comes back at eleven: the 'Stone Unturned'. They were the only one tonight worth listening to."

"Yeah. But maybe we'll catch them some other time."

"It was good to meet you, Alaine. Perhaps we should get together, the four of us…next weekend?"

"Sure, Suzanne. How about it, Nick? Anything planned for next Saturday?"

"Not a thing, far as I know. What did you have in mind?"

"A picnic, maybe, and a swim. Do you feel up to walking a few miles?"

"How few?"

"Down to the old quarry off Forest Drive."

"Never been there."

"Most people haven't. It's far enough from campus not many know about it, but near enough that we don't need a car. Secluded. And it's beautiful!"

"Sounds all right to me. Suzanne?"

"I would love to. I have not been swimming

since…since I left Paris, except for once in the public pool in Arborville." She made a face. "There was too much chlorine, and it was very crowded. I never went back."

"Jack?"

"I'm not in very good shape: haven't gotten much exercise the last few years. But I'm game if everybody else is."

"Fine! Then we'll plan on it. Where shall we meet?"

"In the lobby of Farrington Hall. That's closest, so it'll be a shorter walk…"

"For you, sure! You live right there! …No, *Rom*-lady, just kidding. It's a good place to meet. At nine?"

"Nine or nine-thirty. Let's each bring our own lunch. Then, if we like, we can swap off." She reached for the wine bottle and hefted it: still more than half full. "And I'll make sure this gets there too."

"Won't they give us a hassle? Men, hanging out in the women's dorm?"

"I'll come down to the lobby at nine, so if there's any problem I can vouch for you."

"We'll see you there, then. And now we really do need to go."

Suzanne and I left the booth, found our waitress, and paid the bill. I walked her back to Charlie Blake's house, and she unlocked the door with the key he'd given her. "Jack, thank you for everything. It has been a busy day…but a pleasant one. And I will miss you…as a couch-mate!"

"We'll be seeing each other, I'm sure…"

"Yes, but it will not be the same. Jack, come here."

And her arms went around me, and her face turned up. For an instant our lips brushed, but then she pulled away. "No, Jack, no more. I am not yet ready… I am sorry."

"That's all right. Shake hands, then?"

She smiled, extending hers, and we shook. "See you next weekend, then. If not before!"

4 Hadrian

May 17-21, 1971

That week was a busy one. My first classes started at eight each morning, and the breaks before my later ones I spent in the Research Library: reading Doctor Knight's suggested articles, finding others on related subjects, and adding and adding and adding to my master diagram.

I had four-hour laboratory sessions on Tuesday and

Thursdays: one for Doctor Knight's course, the other for Analytical Chemistry. On Mondays, Wednesdays and Fridays Doctor Knight would expect me to work those same hours, two to six, in his own research laboratory adjoining his office: Room 225, a place some students less fortunate than I called the "Holy of Holies".

It was a well-equipped laboratory, though a little antiquated: long and narrow like my dormitory room, with windows at one end and doors to his office and the corridor at the other. Down one side ran a built-in workbench topped with black imitation slate, with cabinets underneath, a sink set into the middle, and shelves of reagent bottles above. The other side held a small refrigerator, a fume hood, and, next to the windows, a scarred wooden desk which was to be mine.

Since my research plan wasn't yet complete, much less approved by the great man, I couldn't start on the synthesis. Instead, the master assigned me to help prepare materials and "maintain the lab in a safe and usable condition" for his own research.

I washed glassware. I tested the safety shower, and took the extinguisher down to the fire station for inspection. I sorted and inventoried the contents of the shelves and cabinets, compared them with a list Doctor Knight had given me, made up the deficiencies from the organic stockroom down the hall and the larger main stockroom downstairs, and began weeding out those whose expiration dates had passed. Dressed in a lab coat and industrial safety goggles – since the great man had judged the lighter, more comfortable ones I'd brought from Rutgers inadequate – I purified solvents by distillation, and refined solid reagents by dissolving them, filtering, and cooling them in the refrigerator to recrystallize.

So passed my afternoons. And in the evenings I studied, there at the old wooden desk, returning to Holbrook Hall only to sleep. So I hardly noticed the changes which, step by step, were taking place in the room I shared with Hadrian Marsan…until coming back late on Friday night, I opened the door into black light and acid rock.

He'd completely changed the room. The overhead lights were out; the room was flooded with dim purple instead from the tubes of a black-light lamp, the single bright spot a candle on Hadrian's desk. Fluorescent posters hung on all the walls, even those over my own bed, shining yellow and green and red and blue in the darkness.

A spread patterned in black and fluorescent orange covered his bed now, glowing like burning coals. Dim shapes turned above it: mobiles of wire and balsa and shiny foil rotating in the slight draft from the window, reflecting sudden gleams of this or that color from poster or bedspread, candle flame or purple lamp. The pilot lights and illuminated dial of a radio-stereo set shone from his desk beside the candle holder. From the speakers, the music of Jimi Hendrix was pouring: not loudly, but with enough volume to drown out most of the dormitory background noises.

In the middle of this hippie haven, by the light of his one candle, Hadrian was calmly studying: books and papers spread out before him, slide rule in hand. "Hey there, Jack. You're back early!"

"I decided I'd study some other time. What have you done to the room?"

"Fixed it like my room in Marion Hall last year. Not as good, but it'll do for the summer. Like it?"

"I'm not sure. How can you see?"

"With my eyes! Yours will adapt, don't worry." He made a slight adjustment to the slide rule, held it close to the flame and squinted at it, then wrote down a number on the paper in front of him. "Of course, to read, you'd better get close to the candle. Do you need another one?"

"No, I guess not... These are strange posters."

Water, having fallen and turned a mill wheel, flowed away downhill in a stone trough yet somehow wound up above the wheel to fall again and again. Two hands emerged from a drawing tablet, each grasping a pencil and drawing the other. In a room of tangled stairways three sets of faceless figures climbed and descended…each set calling a different direction "down."

"They're Escher designs."

"Who's Escher?"

"Maurits Cornelius Escher: a Dutch artist. They're visual paradoxes. Do you like them?"

"I'm not sure. They remind me of a weird thing one of my friends back home used to draw: a square bar on one end, bent like a horseshoe, that somehow turned into three round rods at the other."

He rose and took a notebook from the shelf, opened it, rummaged among loose papers. "This?"

I held it closer to the candle. "Yes." His was more skillfully done; the square section was shaded to make it look three-dimensional, the round parts drawn as open, hollow pipes. Their ends were even threaded. "What is it?"

"It's a 'poyt': another paradox picture. And here's another: a 'Freemish cube'…" and he turned the page to show the framework of a wooden crate, just as meticulously drawn and shaded…with its furthest corner somehow in front of the nearest.

"And this one, the Penrose Tribar…." It was like the watercourse at the mill reduced to its simplest elements: just a triangle of square beams. My eye followed the perspective along each side, progressively leading away into the picture…and was abruptly back at its starting point. "Kind of blows your mind, doesn't it?"

I was trying to spot the flaw in the Triangle's perspective. "This thing doesn't make sense."

"It isn't supposed to. It's like a Zen riddle. It only makes **non-**sense."

"Zen Buddhism?"

Hadrian's grin glowed pale green in the darkness, like the smile of the Cheshire cat. "Another road to that quantum realm, where something can be true and false at the same time. Like the wave theory of light."

"Huh?"

"Didn't Rutgers teach you the particle-wave duality?"

"Yeah, I had that in sophomore physics. Light acts like a wave sometimes, and like a solid particle other times."

"Yep. This black light, for instance…" He reached out and stroked the air as if gathering cobwebs, then rubbed his fingers together. "An atom of mercury, inside the tube, spits it out like a bullet. But then you can put it through polarizers, or a diffraction grating, and obviously it's a wave. It hits the fluorescent paint on one of these posters…and wham! It's a bullet again and it ricochets, losing energy to become visible light.

"You can't explain fluorescence by the wave theory, and you can't explain polarization with bullets. So light is somehow both at once. A 'wavicle'. What we see, depends on which experiment we run.

"Take that line of reasoning a step further, and you can see nothing's quite what we think it is." He stamped on the floor: "Solid? No, just whirling electrons and other gunk, with empty space in between." Then gathered another handful of air, holding it up for inspection: "But what's 'empty' mean? It means 'chock-full of wavicles.' Virtual particles. Vacuum energy!"

All this, much as it might concern a senior in physics, seemed to have little relevance to my chemist's tidy world of crystals and solvents. "So?"

"So, there's room for lots of things that aren't in the textbooks. Reality's imaginary!"

"Maybe technically. It's a pretty good approximation, though…"

"But wait! There's more! Schrödinger's Equation says everything has a wave function: a cloud of probabilities all around, like a spread-out ghost of itself. So your wave function, right now, overlaps the wave function of everything else that exists. Or ever has. Or ever will.

"And they all interact, forward and backward and sideways through time! So if you knew how, you could detect them and interpret them. You could read somebody's mind, or sense things beyond stone walls, or predict the future. Or push back with your wave function against other things, and move them around without touching them. Control dice, or a roulette wheel…"

"I know, Hadrian. I read science fiction too."

"It isn't fiction! I've seen it! Telepathy, clairvoyance, precognition, telekinesis: they all exist! Rhine proved it in the Fifties, and I'll prove it again if you like. Right here in this room!"

"You're on. Show me!"

"It'll have to be clairvoyance if that's all right with you. I've gotten good scores on that before, and it doesn't need any special concentration from you."

"Sure. What should I do?"

He rose. "Take these cards…"

"Hadrian, I'm buried in cards lately. What kind are these?" Unlike Alaine's they were plain, simple things: one side white, the other bearing a design in black. There weren't many, either, just a couple of dozen.

"Zener cards: the kind Rhine used. Shuffle them, then I'll try to guess the order they're in…"

"All right." Taking them, I turned over a few to look at the designs: a square, a cross, wavy lines…

"No, don't concentrate. Just shuffle."

So I complied, while Hadrian drew copies of each

of the five designs on a sheet of paper. "Now what? Do I let you 'pick a card, any card'?"

"Something like that. Just fan them out…that's right. Face down. And I'll take them out one at a time, and say what I think they are, and put them in five different piles. Then when they're all called, we'll check to see how I did."

"Let's make one change. You touch the card and say what you think it is. Then **I'll** pull it out, and put it on the pile."

"Fine. Ready?"

"Ready."

His hand moved back and forth, as mine had over Alaine's cards…and picked one. "Circle." Taking it out, then, I laid it on the sheet beside the circle he'd drawn.

"Star… Waves… Cross… Circle… Square…" We went through the whole deck, separating them into five piles. "Okay: how many did I get right?"

"One 'circle.' No 'squares' at all. Two 'stars.' One 'wave'…and three 'crosses.' Seven correct, out of twenty-five."

"Pure chance would predict just five, on average."

"So? You lucked into two extras. What does that prove?"

"Nothing, yet. Now, though, we get out the tables I worked out from Rhine's formulas…and here, you see five cards would put me in the fiftieth percentile: just average. Seven cards? By chance I'd score that well, or better, about once in six tries."

"Just luck, Hadrian. Try it again."

"I've done it dozens of times, Jack, alone or with other people helping. Let me see how I'm doing now..." and pulling out another sheet with running totals on it, he began adding to it in pencil.

"This is my nineteenth try since I started recording. Four hundred seventy-five guesses, so far...and a hundred twenty-four hits. On the average, there should have been ninety-five. So I'm twenty-nine hits ahead of the game."

"Still just luck. How many per run, on the average?"

He grabbed the slide rule. "Six point five three...about six and a half. I can usually get at least six; often, seven or eight. And once, I got ten!"

"Big deal, Hadrian. So you can guess a little better than average. But you're missing a lot more than you get right."

"Doesn't matter! The results still add up. Nineteen runs would have a sigma of..." he worked some more with the slide rule... "... three point three two. My best yet!"

"That's all gibberish to me. What does 'sigma' mean?"

"A measure of probability. Random series follow

what statisticians call a 'bell curve'..."

"The kind they use to 'curve' grades?"

"Yep. Graph the test grades in a big class. The graph will be bell-shaped: tall at the center but trailing off to right and left. Like this." He drew a quick sketch of the curve.

"Sigma is a measure of how wide the 'bell' is...." And he added two vertical lines to the sketch, one at each side. "About two-thirds of the grades will be within one sigma of the average. A sixth will be better, and a sixth will be worse."

"So you'd score one 'sigma' above chance, about a sixth of the time?"

"If there were no wave-function effects. But I'm at almost three and a third sigmas." Consulting another table, he twiddled with the slide rule some more. "That would happen just once in...about fifteen hundred tries." He added one more vertical line, far off to the right and extremely short.

"Do you mean it would take fifteen hundred Hadrians, guessing as many cards as you have, for just one to do that well by chance?"

"That's right. In the Rhine work, they accepted one in two hundred as 'proof': two point six sigma. I broke that on my eleventh run. ...So, are you convinced now?"

"No. 'Proof' like this is like 'proof' a given number

won't come up twice in a row on the roulette wheel. It's a pretty good bet, but not scientifically rigorous."

"Neither are the Gas Laws, Jack, but every freshman in Chem 101 has to learn them. They say a gas will do this or that when it's heated or compressed. But it's statistical, just like this: the total of millions of lesser events, collisions between molecules. Quantum events…and we only see the average. But with a big enough sample, it's all the proof you could ever need!"

I'd spotted a possible flaw, though, in his methods. "I know you wouldn't do it consciously – at least, I hope not! But could you be seeing clues on the cards themselves? Dirt-spots, or creases or something, that help you recognize some of them?"

"I thought of that. So I've done it blindfolded a few times, and it made no difference. I still scored sixes and sevens."

"To have it really airtight, you need some way of 'reading' the cards…or something…without seeing them at all, or touching them."

He gave another Cheshire grin. "Great! Can you help me work that out?"

"Hadrian, I don't have much time. Doctor Knight…"

"Oh, I know. He gave you the scholarship, and now he thinks he owns you."

"It isn't that, exactly. But I owe it to him, now, to

do my best."

"Of course. But if you think of some way, please let me know!"

"Sure. I'll keep it in mind."

So as Hadrian turned back to his physics problems, wielding pencil and slide rule in the light of his solitary candle, I lay back on my bed, pondering the things we'd discussed and trying to picture the universe as he must see it: a place of tangible energy and tenuous matter, of shadowy wave-functions and paradoxes. Like the little mill in the poster, with its water falling and falling and falling. Falling…

5 Back Roads

May 22, 1971

Then sunshine was in my eyes. I opened them, squinting against the glare and wishing the window faced any direction but east.

Hadrian was gone. I lay on the bed uncovered, still in the rumpled clothes I'd worn all day Friday, my watch still on my wrist. Groggily I focused my eyes on it.

Eight-forty! They'd be expecting me, Suzanne and the others, at Farrington Hall in twenty minutes…and it was probably at least a fifteen-minute walk. Well, I might be a little late.

I rose, quickly brushed my teeth and hair, put on fresh deodorant, then dug down through my socks and underwear to find my swim trunks. Good old faithful, navy blue shorts with the white trim: I'd had them since high school, though a couple of years had gone by since I'd last worn them. Shaking them out, I stepped in and started to pull them up.

They were very tight now. Had I really put on that much weight these past two years? Tugging hard, I felt a rear seam start to give. All the chlorine in the pool at Rutgers, I thought, must have weakened it. But its parting had relieved the stress. The trunks, at least, were on me now, and only the one seam had torn.

Reaching back to check the tear by feel, I found at least the Nylon liner still intact. It would be embarrassing, but at least my modesty would be safe! So I'd wear them just for today, I decided. If Alaine's quarry seemed worth a second trip, I could buy new trunks for next time.

Pulling on jeans over them, I put on a short-sleeved shirt and got out a clean towel. Wednesday night I'd bought some cheese crackers, a can of Pepsi and a Pluto Pie – raspberry this time – from the machines in the Student Union. Lest any be lost I wrapped them in the towel to make a bundle, and with that under my arm and the campus map in hand, I set out again.

It was a beautiful day, clear and already quite warm, the sun's heat on my shoulders predicting another scorcher like the past half-week's. Already I could feel myself beginning to sweat. I wasn't used to this Southern climate yet, and today I wouldn't have Stanford Hall's air conditioning to protect me!

The map showed me the shortest route lay over the top of College Hill, across Plowman Ellipse and the green park inside it, full of huge old oaks. Their shade brought a welcome respite from the sun in my eyes and on my shoulders. Beyond, the tall white South Campus dorms stood like vast pinstriped dominoes awaiting the push of God's own finger. Detouring the fenced-off construction zone around Lyman Hall, I headed for the easternmost of the four.

White concrete pillars ran unbroken from top to ground, emphasizing its height. I couldn't tell at first how many floors it had; the windows were dark, the panels between them black. Glass doors opened to a lobby filling the entire ground floor save for elevator shafts flanking an exposed stairway with wide, varnished steps. Couches, chairs and low tables were scattered here and there: some occupied, most not.

It looked nothing whatsoever like a prison.

Hands waved from a group of chairs near the entrance. They were all there, Alaine and Nick and Suzanne, with bundles of their own. "We were starting to think you'd decided to stay and do chemistry instead!"

"Sorry about that. I overslept."

"No problem. Would have waited another five minutes or so. Maybe ten… You ready to go, Suzanne? Alaine?"

We headed out again, down the wooded slope behind the dorms toward Calhoun Inlet. Off to our right, I could see the little Student Union beach. Already the shore was dotted with sunbathers, and heads bobbed inside the perimeter of floats. Faintly we could hear the blare of radios, and occasional shouts as swimmers splashed each other. "Why not just go over there?"

Alaine made a face. "Too crowded. And we wanted some exercise, didn't we?"

"I guess so. What's so great about that quarry, though?"

"It's beautiful. It has sheer cliffs coming down to the water, and trees all around. Not like that place over there, all muddy, with no shade and too many people. And it's quiet: no radios, nobody yelling…"

So we continued, following a faint path along the shore, to where a paved road crossed the narrow end of

The Moon Path

Calhoun Inlet on a bridge. "This is Forest Drive. It runs south for miles through University land, and on down through Mannheim State Forest. We can follow it most of the way to the quarry. Or, take the scenic route up over Harrison Point." Alaine smiled. "That's a great spot for parking – I've done it a time or two myself – but there shouldn't be many people there this time of day. And there's a wonderful view across the lake, with the Blue Ridge beyond."

"Is it much further?"

"Maybe an extra half-mile. We'll cut through the woods, and pick up Forest Drive again further on."

My ears pricked up at the promise of shade. "Fine. Let's go!"

Beyond the inlet the shore grew steep and the path divided, one branch climbing along the brink of what soon became tall cliffs of stone and clay. By the time it passed the Student Union beach it must have risen fifty feet or more. I was puffing by then, my body scolding me for the past years of sedentary studying. From that height, though, the swimming area's muddy, crowded water looked completely uninviting.

The path continued to rise, turning back from the brink into the forest. By then I was sweating hard despite the shade, and my trunks were starting to chafe. I was about to ask for a rest break when I noticed light between the trees ahead. Soon we came out again into the open: a picnic area, rustic tables well-shaded under pines and oaks. To our left lay a graveled parking area, though now empty of cars. To the right a line of iron posts, chains stretching from one to the next, barred us from the cliff's edge. A weathered sign facing the tables read "Harrison Point."

Walking to the posts and chains, we gazed out and down. Perhaps a hundred feet below us the lake sparkled, its water coffee-dark behind the reflections of sun and sky. Far out a motorboat moved, trailing white. Wooded hills rose green beyond, dotted with shadows of little fair-weather clouds, while further still great rounded mountains made a bumpy horizon.

Suzanne was entranced. "It is all so beautiful, so peaceful!" She slowly lifted her gaze from lake, to hills, to peaks beyond. "The mountains, especially. Someday, I would like to visit them."

"Don't you have mountains in France? The Alps, and the Pyrenees?"

"Yes, but I was never able to go there. When I lived in Mortagne, there was never the money. And after that, there was never the time!"

"Maybe, one of these weekends, we can get up an expedition."

"Jack, you were telling us about collecting rocks in Franklin, New Jersey." Alaine smiled. "Did you know we have a Franklin here, too, in North Carolina? With famous rocks of its own?"

"No. What kind?"

"There are ruby mines in Cowee Valley, up above: open, for a fee, to whoever wants to sift through the gravel and keep what they find. I had a boyfriend my freshman year, before I met Carl: a geology major. He gave me a little vial of stones they'd collected there on a field trip. I think I still have it somewhere."

"I'd like to see those. And maybe, some weekend before the summer's over, we can go up and try our own luck. Is it far?"

"Sixty or seventy miles, I guess. An hour and a half's drive; maybe two hours. The mountain roads are kind of twisty."

"But we can't all fit on Nick's bike…"

"We could take a bus, I guess."

"I **hate** buses! I rode the bus here from Arborville and a man sat down beside me, and was smoking a cigarette, and would not stop bothering me. When he left I put my suitcase there, so no one else would come."

"Then maybe we can borrow a car. Charlie Blake's?"

"Perhaps. I will ask him. Or perhaps he would like to come along…"

"If he wants to. We can make more definite plans later, when we have a better handle on some transportation. In the meantime, let's enjoy the view from here. Can you see the Sleeping Giant?"

"The what?"

Alaine pointed. "The Sleeping Giant. See, that mountain with the three peaks is the head: forehead, nose, and chin. Then the one beside it, with the long curved top, is the chest. And 'way over there, those two peaks are the feet sticking up."

"I see it now. Wow! It really does look like somebody lying on his back, with the other mountains around him. How big would he have to be, though?"

"I don't know. Ten or twenty miles tall, I guess."

"Let's hope he never wakes up, then. There'd be earthquakes…"

"Or worse. There's an old Indian legend I found in a book in the library. One of their gods rebelled during creation, like Satan in the Old Testament. To keep him from ruining everything they'd made, the other gods wove a net from stars and threw it over him while he slept. Until the stars fade, then, he'll go on sleeping…and be part of this view."

We leaned on the posts, and gazed out into the distance in silence…until the morning's peace was shattered by an approaching car, muffler faulty and radio playing loudly. "Uh-oh. First customer of the day!"

Alaine made a disgusted face. "Some people just

can't stand quiet. Well, let's move on. It's always quiet at the quarry."

So while the newcomers parked and unloaded, setting up their own picnic at one of the tables – leaving the car radio blasting through open windows all the while – we headed on across the gravel and back into the shade. A gently descending slope brought us, after another half-mile or so, back to Forest Drive. Facing us across it another road, unpaved and barred by a chain slung between iron posts, led off into deep forest. "Where does this go?"

"Probably to an experimental plot in the woods. The Forestry Department does studies on different types of trees: how fast they grow; how they stand up to insects, drought, and so on. Some of these go on down to the water, but the University blocked them off years ago. I think they were worried people'd go swimming, and drown, and there'd be lawsuits."

"Does that mean we're trespassing?"

Alaine smiled. "Not until we get to the quarry road."

"What happens if they catch us?"

"Probably nothing. I've heard the forestry students come out sometimes to party. It isn't approved by the Department, but it goes on." We rounded one more gentle curve, and she pointed. "There it is. ...But what's this? They've taken down the chain!"

The two iron posts were there, flanking the weed-choked road about fifty feet from the edge of the pavement. The chain was missing…but, no. It hung from one post only, most of its length buried in mud and dead leaves. The ring welded to the other post was empty.

Nick bent and examined the road surface. "Doesn't look like it's traveled much, though. No tire tracks since the rain last week. And the chain…" He lifted it free of the litter which covered it. "Alaine, this has been down for months."

"You're right. I haven't been here since last fall. It was up, then…but it could have fallen any time since."

Nick had spotted something else among the rotting leaves at the base of the chainless post. "Aha!" He straightened, holding it up. "Look at this." It was an old padlock, open and very rusty. The shackle resisted his efforts to turn it, and wouldn't close at all. "Looks like somebody hit the chain and it broke. Guess time and weather did the rest."

"Nobody must have cared much, or they'd have replaced it."

"Shall we go?"

"After you, my Lady." And dropping the rusted lock back into the litter, Nick followed her across the fallen chain.

6 The Quarry

May 22, 1971

The new road led off through deep shade, curving gently now and again. It had seen a lot of traffic once; the wheel tracks were worn deep. Now, though, tall weeds grew between them. Clearly few cars had come this way in months, perhaps in years.

"You know," Nick mused as we walked, "we ought to replace that lock."

"Why?"

"Sooner or later, somebody else'll notice the chain's down. Especially now that summer's here. And either the University'll put a new lock on, or people will start coming…and maybe Alaine's quarry will get as crowded as the Student Union beach."

"Perish the thought!"

"Sorry, *Rom*-lady. So let's keep it private; let's make it 'our' private. If we want the chain down, we can take it down. Otherwise, it'll be up!"

She smiled, nodding. "Do you have a padlock? One that's not too shiny and new?"

"Got an old combination lock at the trailer somewhere. I'll see if I can find it. Maybe spray some brown paint on it: make it look as rusty as the old one. Like it'd been there for years."

"Good. I'll feel better about this place if it's not just open to whoever comes along."

Suzanne was looking from one to the other, incredulous. "Do you mean that you will lock up the University's property, with your own lock? But that is wrong!"

"Why?"

"What will happen if they want to use it for something?"

"Way I see it, they want it locked up so people won't come in. If we put another lock on, we're just putting it back the way they wanted it."

"Nick, you're what Carl calls a 'barracks lawyer.' That may not be true, but it sounds good. Maybe it would even convince a jury."

"With luck, it won't have to. Just have to be careful not to leave fingerprints in the paint!"

We pushed through the weeds for another quarter-mile or so, rounding a couple of gentle curves. Then Alaine pointed again, this time to a large dead oak with a hole in it. "That's the landmark I was looking for. Now we leave the newer road…and I hope I can find the way again. The old quarry road has gone pretty much back to nature."

The deep wheel tracks we'd been following branched off now from what was clearly a newer road continuing downslope, perhaps to the shore of the lake. The forest had taken back that older way, hidden it under shrubs and fallen leaves. Trees grew between the ruts, many as large as those to the sides. Even the narrow path among them was weed-choked, clearly disused. "How long has this place been abandoned, anyway? And how did you find out it was here?"

"Since the Civil War, maybe. My old boyfriend I told you about – Julian, who gave me the rubies – brought me here the first time. He'd found it on some map from the 1850s or so. There probably aren't many others who know about it. I've come a few times since, and I've never seen anybody else or signs they'd been here lately. Not even litter."

"Sounds like a good place for skinny-dipping."

She laughed. "That was what Julian had planned. Among other things!"

"It was just a thought, *Rom*-lady…"

"What is… 'skinny dipping'? An American custom?"

"Maybe. Swimming without a suit: 'dipping,' in just your skin."

I remembered the YMCA pool in Camden, and a swimming course one summer in grade school. Trunks had been forbidden since the fibers they shed might clog the filters. Surrounded by others my age, I'd "skinny-dipped" without concern. I'd only been eight that year, though, and there'd been no girls in the class.

By age twelve, though, as my body changed I found myself grown oddly bashful. Even camping with the Pioneer Boys that summer, when at a deep-woods swimming hole some others had shed all their clothes, that new modesty had kept my own trunks on.

And what, too, of the law? New Jersey's were strict, classing any nudity before non-consenting witnesses as "lewd conduct" punishable by fines or prison. Some high-school friends had accidentally broken those laws in Rancocas Park, stumbled on by another couple who'd surely come with similar plans. "Non-consenting"? Luckily the judge had doubted that, and Bert and Cathy had gotten off with a stern lecture and a warning.

This place, though, seemed far from potential witnesses, consenting or otherwise. "What's the law like, here? In South Carolina?"

Alaine laughed. "Stupid. Vague and stupid; it means whatever the judge wants it to. But they've got to catch you. And out here…?" She gestured at the woods around us. " 'Wild and lone' !" Something in her voice made those final words sound like a quotation.

Suzanne looked contemplative. "In the pool in Paris, we never wore suits. That was where Reesh…where I learned. Great-Aunt Clarisse had to buy me a suit so that we could go to the pool in Arborville." She patted her towel-wrapped bundle. "But I have worn it only that one time. It is very uncomfortable."

"I can sympathize. I wore my trunks under these jeans, but they're old and too tight. I tore a seam getting them on. Not comfortable either." An understatement; the chafing was downright painful now, one thigh smarting as if already rubbed raw. Modesty or none, losing these trunks was starting to seem like a really good idea.

"You wouldn't want to get sunburned, though."

"But at the quarry, there's plenty of shade…"

"Tell you what, *Rom*-lady. We'll vote when we get there. If everybody agrees, we will. But only if everybody agrees!"

"Sure! 'An ye hurt none, do as ye will'…"

"What was that?"

"Something my Aunt Theda used to say: an old proverb, sort of. 'If it doesn't hurt anybody, do whatever you like'!"

"Well, hold onto that thought! …How much farther is it now?"

"I don't remember, exactly. And you can't really see it 'til you're almost to the edge… There!"

Granite had once been dug here, but decades must have passed since then. No machinery remained, no buildings or walls, just a big open pit perhaps a hundred feet square with gray stone sides sheer as the cliffs of Harrison Point. No iron posts, no safety chain guarded the brink; only a rim of bare rock and thin, weed-grown soil marked it off from the forest around it.

Stepping to the edge, I looked down. Small trees grew here and there on the sides, rooted in crevices of the rock. A larger fissure split the wall to my left: five or six feet wide at the top, half-filled with broken rock and weeds and shadows. Reaching out from the main pit, it gradually narrowed to vanish among the trees.

I couldn't tell the pit's true depth, for water partly filled it. The surface lay perhaps a dozen feet below the rim where we stood. But unlike the big lake, brown with mud, this water was transparent and faintly blue, the jumbled rockpiles at its corners clearly visible as they continued down beneath. "Why is it so clear? Is it spring-fed?"

"I think so. Maybe water started coming up, and that's why they abandoned it in the first place. And there aren't any swimmers here, either, stirring up mud from the bottom."

In the far corner a shelf jutted out, a couple of feet above the water: big enough, I thought, to hold a small house. "What's that?"

"That's where we're headed." Alaine started off around the pit's rim, talking as she went. "I think it's where the hoist was mounted, to lift out the blocks of stone. There are holes where big bolts must have held it down."

At the corner of the pit a crude, steep stairway had been hacked from the stone. Taking her towel-bundle between her teeth Alaine went down it backward, using both hands to steady herself. "Come on down! It's easier than it looks."

One by one we made the descent: Nick, then I, and finally Suzanne. "Alaine, you were right. This place is beautiful!"

Trees overhung the platform, pine and oak and hickory, dappling it in green-tinted shade. Where sunlight struck the broken stone it glittered with mineral grains. Soil had gathered along the base of the wall, and grass and wildflowers had taken root. Across from us the walls were still in shadow, though bushes here and there were beginning to catch the sun. The water faithfully reflected this study in gray and green, making the old quarry seem bottomless with a second bright blue sky somewhere far below.

Pulling off her shoes and socks, Alaine dangled her feet in the water. "Just right: not too warm, and not too cold!" She kicked out, splashing water in all directions. Ripples spread out across the surface, gradually fading. "Well, Nick," she added after a minute, "do I have to put on my suit for this or not?"

"Let's find out. We can do a nickel-and-penny vote…"

"What's that?"

"Secret-ballot vote we'd use when somebody wanted to join the bike club. Everybody starts with a nickel and a penny. Pass around a box, and everybody drops one in: the nickel for 'yes', the penny for 'no.' When the box comes back, you look inside. If it's all nickels, no pennies, the new man is in. If there's even one penny, he's out…but nobody'll ever know who voted against him."

"That's like how Aunt Theda told me the Masons used to vote, long ago: with black balls and white ones, though, instead of coins. It's where the term came from, to 'blackball' somebody."

"Probably the same thing. One black ball and you're out?"

"Yes. I guess a good system never dies; it just changes with the centuries." She winked at him, and he nodded.

"Well, I've got plenty of change." I reached into my pocket. "Is there anybody here who doesn't?"

"I did not bring my purse today, so, yes, I need it. I will give back the one…no. I will give you back six cents, Jack, sometime next week."

"You don't have to pay me back, Suzanne."

"But I will. Just to keep myself honest."

"Okay. Anybody else need some?"

Nobody did. "And what shall we use for the ballot box?"

"I don't know. Too bad nobody remembered to bring any cups!"

"We could split one of the canned drinks, and then use the can…"

"Ucch. Then the coins would be sticky!"

"One of my shoes!" Alaine picked one up and held it out. "It's the right size, and you can't see down into the toe. …It doesn't smell terrible, does it?"

Nick took it, sniffed and made a mock-sour face. "Not terrible," he echoed,with a grin.

"All right. We've got the ballot box, and we've all got ballots. A penny from anybody means 'suits'; all nickels means 'skinny-dip'. Ready?"

"Ready."

"I think…yes. Ready."

"*Rom*-lady, why don't you cast the first one?"

He held up the shoe, toe pointed down. She had a coin in her hand already, its identity hidden by her fingers, and thrust it into the shoe without hesitation. "Done."

"Jack?"

I dropped the nickel in quickly, lest I lose my nerve: the urge to adventure, the torn trunks' chafing – and, to be honest, the eternal male desire to see the opposite sex naked! – having narrowly won out over my own modesty; still half-hoping, though, someone else would put in a penny and outvote me. "Done."

"Suzanne?"

The shoe came to her, and she stood there looking at it for a moment. Glancing down at herself, she made a face…then quickly pushed something into the shoe, drew back her arm, and flung the other coin far out across the water to splash and sink. "Done."

"Back to me…and done. Who wants to count the votes?"

"I will. It's my shoe, after all."

So Alaine turned it up, and poured out into her hand, clinking…four nickels. She held them out to show us all. "Skinny-dip!"

Nick nodded, smiling as he began to unbutton his shirt. " 'Lace and leather lay aside'." With its rhythm and alliteration, that had to be another quote. But from where?

Unzipping my jeans, I started to haul them off… "Damn." I was more nervous than I'd thought; I'd forgotten to take off my shoes first.

Suzanne undid the last button on her skirt, let it slip, then folded it carefully before laying it down again. "Jack, should I turn my back again while you undress?"

"Only if you want to."

"I understand that you are modest, and this is difficult for you."

"It is. But that's something I'd really like to get past." Setting the shoes aside, I got my jeans off on the second try and dropped them in a heap.

Suzanne was already down to panties and brassiere: all bright yellow, like the blouse. She was stocky, but more from heavy bone structure, I thought, than from mere fat. And so very **pink,** all over! A small gold medallion hung around her neck on a chain. "What's that?"

"This? It is a Saint Christopher medal, blessed in church." She held it out to show me. "I wear it always, next to my skin. I like to think that it helped to keep me safe, on my trip to America."

"Very nice." I reached out to take it.

Suzanne shook her head, pulling it away again, though with a smile. "Jack, you are stalling." She rolled her eyes in mock exasperation. "Are you going to stand there all day, in your shirt and your socks and those torn-up trunks?"

"Sorry." I started on my shirt buttons, deliberately keeping my gaze down-turned as I continued to undress. Even so, I was almost painfully conscious of Suzanne's movements as she took off the brassiere, pushed down the panties and stepped out of them. Somehow I managed to finish my own undressing before I looked back at her.

"There. Was that so difficult?" She was standing facing me, hands on her hips, wearing only her medal. Her breasts were large and soft, with low but prominent nipples...

I blushed, feeling an erection starting. With some effort I tore my gaze back up to her face: at the same time thinking hard about ice, about snowdrifts, about the pain in my feet from walking through them, about anything that might distract and pacify the little rebel down below. Thoughts of cold, I'd learned in adolescence, worked best. *Ice and snow…*

"Poor Jack. Have you never seen a woman before?"

"I've never seen you before, like this." I smiled, trying to hide my embarrassment. "But I like what I see. A lot!"

"Oh, Jack. But there is such a lot of me!" She looked down at herself, clutched at her belly. "I bulge, all over. And sag!"

"Not so much. You look like somebody in a Rubens painting: 'Woman About to Bathe in a Flooded Quarry'."

She smiled. "Is there such a painting?"

"I don't think so. But if I were Rubens right now, I'd be setting up my easel."

"You are not merely being kind?"

"Suzanne, I like you. I like you as a person…and I like the package it comes in, too."

"Thank you, Jack. I still do not completely believe you. But thank you, just the same.

"And now, I am ready to swim!" Turning away, she took three steps and hurled herself in a horizontal dive from the slab's edge.

Nick and Alaine were already in the water, and Alaine called to me. "Come on in; it's fine!"

So I walked to the edge and climbed down slowly over the jumbled rocks beyond it, next to the quarry wall. The surface layer was warm, but underneath it the water was frigid. I lowered myself slowly into it.

"You know, it's easier if you jump!"

"Maybe. But I'll get there. Give me time!"

"You'll be there all day at this rate! Let me help." Alaine drew back one arm and splashed a sheet of water at me.

Suzanne surfaced, far out in the pool. "Jack, are you stalling again?" She gulped air and submerged. Seconds later, something grabbed both my ankles and pulled. Suddenly my head was underwater.

I broke away, kicking, and found precarious footing on a slippery, angled rock, getting my face clear again. "What the hell?"

There was a stir ten feet in front of me, and Suzanne's head appeared. "See? It is much better, once you are down in the water."

"You didn't have to try to drown me!"

"You would not have drowned: not if you can stand up in the water, with your head out. Come on out and swim. I will not drown you, I promise!" She inhaled and went under again, quickly reappearing another ten feet out.

The water didn't seem nearly so cold now that I was in it. Tentatively I pushed off from the rock and began a slow sidestroke, heading for the far side of the quarry as if swimming across that pool in Camden.

It seemed like a long way. But Suzanne paced me,

moving silently through the water until we came to the far side.

I was winded by the time we reached it. Every muscle seemed to ache, and my old back injury was throbbing again. My heart was pounding in my ears, and faintly I could even hear the murmur of the defective heart valve which had helped save me from joining Carl in Viet Nam.

Gasping, I groped with my feet for another rock to stand on. "I had no idea I was so out of shape!"

Suzanne shook her head. "You swim the hard way, Jack. You use up all of your strength in fighting the water. Ree...my teacher said that to swim well you must work with the water, and let it work with you, as a fish or a dolphin does."

"How?" Finding a foothold at last, I stood up.

"First: why do you stay on the top of the water?"

"So I can breathe!"

"Can you not hold your breath for very long?"

"Yeah, I guess."

"Then let us sit, and rest for a while. And then, when you have your breath back, we will try something a little different." Kicking backward, she lifted herself with her hands to sit chest-deep on a large rock below the surface, her shoulders in warm sunlight skimming down the quarry wall. "Join me?"

Climbing carefully onto the slippery stone, I turned

to sit beside her.

The water, so still and smooth a few minutes before, was all in motion now: stirred to life by our own efforts, and by those of Nick and Alaine as they played together in the deep water off the corner of the platform. It lifted Suzanne's breasts and moved them gently back and forth...

"Jack, can you see underwater?"

Caught! I looked guiltily up at her face. "I...well..." Then I realized her question had nothing to do with what I had been watching. "I don't know. The water in the pools where I've swum before always burned my eyes when I tried."

"Yes; it is the chlorine. The one in Arborville was bad, also. But this is not a public pool..."

"I'll try, then." And taking a deep breath I slid down off the rock again, let my head go under...and looked.

Everything was blurry at first; then gradually my vision cleared. I could see the rocks in front of me, one behind another, going down and down until the faint haze of the water made them mere silhouettes... My lungful of air ran out; I came back up.

"Is it easier here?"

"No burning at all. And I can see a fair distance."

"Then sit, and take your next few breaths very deep...and watch what I do." As I lifted myself back onto the rock she slipped off it, checked to see that I

Jack Peredur

was watching, and ducked under the surface.

Kicking in slow motion, reaching out for the water and thrusting it backward, she swam about ten feet before popping back to the surface. "Did you see what I did?"

"You make it look so easy!"

"It is! Watch again." This time, she swam back to me, surfacing almost in my lap. "There. You saw how. Now try it yourself."

Gamely I went in again. It felt awkward at first, but we both persisted…and then, quite suddenly, it was working! The water and my own momentum carried me smoothly ahead. I opened my eyes again to watch the rocks passing below and Suzanne swimming at my side. Coming up at last for air, I feared the spell might be broken. When I went down again, though, everything still worked.

Suzanne dived beneath me, looked up into my eyes, and smiled. I followed her into the depths until water pressed hard against my eardrums and the light around us was blue. Upward, then, toward the light and the air once more. We surfaced together, laughing, the water buoying us up and the sunlight bright on our water-beaded skins…and dived again, and again.

The quarry's waters were ours now, and held no terrors. Suzanne had taught me the way of the dolphin.

7 Masks

The sun by now had come over the quarry rim, and its granite walls shone and glittered all around us. An hour, or maybe a little more, had passed since first we'd entered the water. Nick and Alaine were taking a break side by side in the shade, their feet in the water, talking. Suzanne and I swam back to them, the full width of the quarry, almost effortlessly. Reluctant now to climb out I found another subsurface rock to sit on, and she settled close beside me.

"Welcome back. We were afraid you'd decided this hole wasn't big enough for the four of us!"

"Suzanne was teaching me to swim."

"You didn't know how?"

I shrugged. "I thought I did. But the instructors at the 'Y' didn't know what Suzanne knows. It took her an hour to show me everything I was doing wrong!"

"Jack was fighting the water as if it were an enemy...."

"...And Suzanne taught me to make friends with it. To work with it, not against it."

"And then, when you learned...?"

"Suddenly, it was easy."

Alaine turned to Nick. "Just what I was saying: we need to work in harmony with the forces in Nature, and in ourselves. And stop thinking we can only make progress by fighting them. Or pretending they're not there!"

"Like one of my friends used to say: 'you need to be a little crazy, or you'll go nuts'!"

"What are you talking about?"

"Masks."

"Masks? Disguises?"

Alaine nodded. "Disguises we all wear, to hide who we really are. Sometimes even from ourselves."

"Do you mean social roles? Or swimsuits?"

"Both, and more. Anything that stands between us and what we could become. Limitations we've been taught to accept, that aren't real. Jack, tell me: how do you feel right now?"

"Great! Why?"

"Aren't you missing something?" Her eyes darted downward, then back up to meet mine again.

"What? Oh, my trunks?"

"Does it bother you?"

"It did at first. I stopped thinking about it, though, while Suzanne was teaching me to swim. Now it doesn't seem to matter much. And they were chafing me pretty badly." I reached down to test the spot with a finger: still sore, though during the swimming lesson I'd forgotten about that as well. "Guess I'm better off without."

Nick smiled at Alaine, leaned close and whispered something into her ear.

She nodded to him and replied. It sounded like another quote: " 'In token your spirit is free as well'."

"What was that?"

"Just a line we both learned once: 'Be free in body, in token your spirit is free as well'."

"Is that from some sort of…nudist tract?"

"'Tract'?" She smiled. "Well…maybe. Have you ever studied the history of religion?"

"Not really. My family were Methodists, but we didn't go much. And I'm afraid I spent a lot of my Sunday-school time daydreaming."

"Oh, the Christians wouldn't have taught you this anyway. You had to wear your 'Sunday best' to church, didn't you?"

"Of course!"

"And the more you'd spent on your clothes, the better?"

"I never really looked at it that way...but yeah, maybe. We couldn't very well go in blue jeans, could we?"

"Why not? Would God have been offended?"

"I doubt it. But the people there would have been upset."

"So it was a status display." She shrugged. "Wrap up in your social role, and put on your mask. Then expect your heart still to be open, with love and charity for all. And wonder why so many Christians are hypocrites!

"The old religion knew you can't hide from the Gods that way. 'As within, so without'." She gestured across the quarry, its waters now still again. "The outside and the inside are like those cliffs and their reflection. So to come before the Gods with your heart open and honest, you should make your outside open and honest too, wearing just what the Gods gave you.

Jack Peredur

What you're wearing right now."

Suzanne was shocked. "But that would be…*sacrilège*! We must always cover ourselves…"

"Except when you're swimming?"

"I…Alaine, I do not know. Is it a sin, what we are doing now?"

"What's a sin?"

"An offense against God, or against another person…"

"Are we offending anybody? Didn't we all put nickels in the shoe?"

Suzanne nodded.

"And how can we hurt God, by being as God made us?"

"Yes. But in a church?"

Alaine laughed. "Who built the church?"

"People made it, to honor God…"

"And who made this place?" She made a sweeping gesture, taking in the water, the cliffs, the trees, the sky.

"God…and the people who dug out the stone."

"So in God's places, if you like, you can wear just God's gifts. But in people's places, you have to wear what people expect you to?"

"Well…yes, I suppose so. But to worship God…"

"How better than in a place God made? And just as God made **you?**"

Suzanne nodded slowly. "Perhaps you are right. But for this to be a church, something still is missing. Surely no priest would hold Mass here. Especially, without wearing any..." she groped in memory for the word. "Any *vêtements*. 'Vestments,' do you say?"

"No Catholic priest would, of course. They're the people who invented 'Sunday best,' I think. You'd have to find a priest of the old religion. ...Or a priestess."

"But that was long ago! There are none now, are there?"

Nick looked at Alaine, and she smiled. "Oh, you might still find one or two."

"And did you say...a priest**ess**? A woman who was also a priest?"

Alaine simply nodded.

"And could that priestess...hear my confession, and forgive my sin?"

"Nobody but you can really forgive you. That's always between you and God, or the Gods, and the person you harmed if there is one. The priestess can only make it a little easier: by listening, and suggesting ways to help make it right again."

Suzanne was struggling with some difficult new concept. "Would such a priestess...admit to any stranger that she was one? Or would she also wear a mask? Except, perhaps, in a place such as this?"

"I'm sure she'd wear a mask, Suzanne. The Old Religions have been persecuted too much, for too many centuries, to be comfortable out in the open now. Except in places 'wild and lone'." Again she gestured to the trees around us. "Like this one."

"Then, how could I be sure that I had found her?"

"How do you know a Christian priest when you see one?"

"By his vestments. And by the fact that I went to the church to find him."

"So: look for the priestess the same way. In a place wild and lone. And wearing the vestments the Gods have given." Alaine swept her hand again at the stone and greenery surrounding us, then down the front of her own body, her eyes emphasizing each gesture.

Grown wide in dawning wonder, Suzanne's eyes followed. "It is you, is it not?"

Our *Rom*-lady nodded, smiling.

"Alaine…" She paused, gathering her courage. "Alaine, will you hear my confession? Can you? And help me to ask for forgiveness?"

"Yes. If you want me to."

"I do. You must. For I can no longer go to the Catholic priests. It…it is too terrible, what I have done."

"Alaine, maybe Nick and I should leave. Isn't confession supposed to be private?" I started to rise…but Suzanne laid a hand on my thigh.

"No, please, Jack. Stay. You also, Nick. I trust you both, and you are my only friends here. You should know what it is that I did. Alaine, is that all right?"

"If that's the way you want it. But I think we should all swear to keep secret what we're about to hear. No matter how bad it is."

We all agreed.

"Let's set up a Circle, then." Alaine rose. "Help me?"

"Sure. What's a Circle?"

"Just a space marked out to work in. Round, traditionally. With markers at the compass points." She studied the scattered rocks on the platform, then stepped a few feet away from us.

"Let's center it right here. We'll need to shift that rock if we can, and that one…and put them there, and over there. They'll do for the North and South points, and that big one is good for the West right where it is. And for the East…I wish that one were bigger, but it'll do for now. We can fix up a better altar some other time."

Nick was single-handedly shifting the first one she'd pointed out, muscles flexing under dark sweat-sheened skin. I attacked the other, and after a moment Suzanne came to help me. It was heavy, but by lifting and sliding one end and then the other, we got it into place. "There. Anything else?"

"We really should have candles on them, but they'll do for now. This isn't a full-scale ritual Circle, and we have Earth and Water and Air. And the Sun, of course, is Fire.

"Let's clear everything out of the middle, now: the rocks and sticks and stuff…. No, Jack: not that one." I'd been about to toss out a three-foot length of sycamore, thick as my thumb and nearly white where most of the bark had shed. "I'll take that. Since I don't have my *athamé* with me…."

"Your what?"

"My blade of power. Normally I'd use that to trace the Circle, but a wand will do as well. And in a pinch, any good solid stick can be a wand." She hefted the branch, then tested it with both hands across her knee. It didn't break. "Yes; this will do nicely."

Carrying it, then, she stepped to the center of the space we'd cleared. "Nick, grab the wine and that Melba toast I brought. And everybody, gather around me."

"How do we do this?"

"First, I'll trace the boundary. If you can, imagine the tip of the wand leaving a trail of white fire behind it. Fire that rises, and forms a thin wall around us."

Lowering its end to the stone she walked slowly clockwise around us, beginning and ending at the East.

I tried to help by visualizing the fire, and found the image came easily. White flames, not quite visible to the outer eye, soon towered around us and merged into a wall of light.

"Next, we call on the Guardians to keep this place safe from any disturbance, physical or spiritual. Some call them the Four Archangels. And when that's done, we tap on the shoulders of the Gods Themselves."

She raised her improvised wand over the waters, like an undraped female Moses about to part the Red Sea. "Guardian of the East! Keeper of the Powers of Air: be present, we pray You, and guard this place from all perils." The tip of the rod flicked in a quick pattern: a five-pointed star drawn in air, starting and ending at the uppermost point. Walking the Circle's rim again, she did the same at the South, the West, and the North in turn: calling upon the Keepers of Fire, of Water and Earth.

Finally we faced the East again, and she raised the wand straight up. "Eternal Gods! Father and Mother of All: be present, we pray You, to witness what shall be done in this place." The rod moved again, but this time the star it traced was six-pointed, directly above our heads. "So mote it be."

Nick echoed, "So mote it be." I repeated the phrase, though not fully understanding what it meant. Was it the Old Religion's "Amen"? Suzanne, last of all, repeated it once again.

Alaine turned back toward us, lowering the wand. "The Circle is sealed; those within it are gathered in the sight of the Gods. Let none leave this place until the Circle is opened. Let none speak unworthily of that which happens within."

Again Nick replied, "So mote it be", and Suzanne and I echoed it.

"Welcome, Jack and Suzanne, to the temple of the Old Religion: a place which is not a place, in a time which is not a time. And welcome, Nick, once again. Though you are not of this faith and bound by no oaths of initiation, still I welcome you all, for the Gods have brought us together."

"Thank you, Alaine."

She gestured toward the ground. "Shall we sit?"

"Is it all right?"

"Sure. You may have noticed, we're not very formal in this church."

So the four of us sat crosslegged in the Circle, facing each other, within the boundary set by the corner stones.

"First, does anybody have questions about what we've done so far?"

Suzanne nodded. "I see why the Four Archangels were called to be around us here. As a child, I was taught to pray that angels be around me as I slept. But why do you call on two Gods: Father and Mother?"

"That's the way God is seen in the Old Religion: because each of us has a father and a mother, and God has the same relation to all living things that parents have to a child. It was only when men became the leaders, and turned women into sex-and-baby machines, that the Mother was forgotten."

"So that now, we say 'God the Father'...but there is no 'God the Mother'? Only the Mother of God... Who is the Virgin Mary!"

"Yes...as the Church sees Her. But originally She was as powerful as the Father, and as important. Neither was complete without the other. And not only Christ, but all of us, are Their children."

"And that is why He told us to pray to...Our Father?"

"Right. Not just His, but everybody's. Because he spoke to Jews, who had forgotten the Mother, He mentioned only the Father. But if you look back a thousand years earlier, at the beginnings of the Jewish faith, the Mother is there too."

"Then, always, when I went into the Lady Chapel and prayed to the Virgin Mary...I was praying to God the Mother, behind a mask?"

"Yes. But now we've taken off our masks. And She's taken off Hers too, for us."

"Then I will pray to Her again, here. But first, I must

make my confession…and be forgiven, if that is possible."

"All right. But I said we needed to swear secrecy, and we haven't done it yet. We agreed to before the Circle was cast, but we should do it formally with the Gods as witnesses.

"We use the Oath of the Sanctuary to guard most of our secrets: all but a few things that could really hurt you, or somebody else, if you tried to use them without the right preparation. I first swore it with Aunt Theda when I was thirteen. And she'd had to swear it with the Gypsies, even after they'd finally come to trust her, before they'd teach her anything at all.

"Will you swear it with me, now?"

We agreed.

"Then repeat after me: I, Alaine…"

"I, Nicholas…"

"I, Suzanne…"

I'd noticed Nick using his given name, so I decided to use mine too. "I, Jason…"

"…Before those assembled here as Witnesses…do solemnly swear, that I will always keep secret…those things entrusted to my ears alone…in this Sanctuary of the Gods…unless it be to another person…properly sworn before these Witnesses.

"And may the powers of my mind turn against me…should I break this solemn Oath.

"So mote it be!"

And we echoed, in unison this time, "So mote it be!"

Alaine looked around at us. "Good. Now, Suzanne, what did you want to say? I can't forgive you by myself. That's between you and the Gods. But maybe I can help as much as the priest of some other religion could."

The French girl took a deep breath, then let it out very slowly. "I..." Her voice was very quiet now, hesitant, pausing in clear dread before each word as her eyes darted from each of us to the next.

"I...murdered...my baby."

8 Richard

May 22, 1971

We all stared at Suzanne, in shock and dismay. **"What?"**

Eyes brimming with tears, she repeated. "I murdered my baby."

"Oh, no. Suzanne, you'd better tell it from the beginning. What baby?"

After swallowing hard a time or two, she went on.

"You knew that I left home, after finishing at the *lycée*, and went to Paris?"

"Yes, you told us. And you got a job, I think, at a dressmaker's shop?"

"I did: a job which paid me well, so that I was able to save money and send some home. My parents had not wanted me to go. But when they saw that I was happy there, and doing well, they grudgingly gave their blessing.

"I had been there about a year when I met Richard." She pronounced his name in the French way, with accent on the second syllable.

"He was the one who taught you to swim?"

"That, and many other things... Richard was from a rich family, and eight years older than I...and very handsome. One day he came into the shop: for no reason, he said, but to see me more closely. I was more attractive then...and not so fat!

"As you say here, he 'swept me off my feet' with compliments and gifts and visits to expensive restaurants. His family had their own swimming pool, and he invited me there. The house was almost his, for they had another in the country and his parents stayed there most of the time. When I said that I could not swim, he offered to teach me...and I accepted.

"The pool was beautiful, though not so lovely as this place: indoors, but separate from the house, with a glass roof to let in the sun. We swam there often, on days when I did not have to work. And though we wore no clothes, no swimsuits, Richard was always a perfect gentleman. He taught me to hold my breath, and dive, and open my eyes, and swim underwater.

"Often I would cook for him afterward. He told me that I was an excellent cook. We would eat together, in the woolly bathrobes which we wore when we left the pool. Then we would dress, and Richard would drive me home.

"But one night – it was a Friday, the week of his birthday – he asked me to stay and help him to celebrate. I had Saturday off as well, so I agreed. No one would miss me if I did not go back to my rooms that night…"

Alaine smiled crookedly. "Uh-oh. Here it comes."

Suzanne nodded. "He opened for us a bottle of brandy. The moon was full, and he suggested that we sit by the pool again and drink it by moonlight. He did not usually allow glass there; it might be broken and cut someone. But that night, he said, was special. So we took the bottle, and went to sit side by side on the diving board.

"I had not had brandy before, and I drank far too much. It made me very drunk, and a little sleepy. I remember lying back on the diving board. Then my robe was open, and he was touching me as no one ever had before: touching me all over, with fingers and lips and tongue. I knew that it was wrong, but somehow I no longer cared.

"That was the first of many nights which we spent together. Richard taught me many ways to make love. He liked… But that is not important any longer; he is gone. Let me say, only, that finally he made me pregnant.

"I was so happy, for I believed that the new life was sacred. I thought that it would make him happy also, for he was the father. He had said, from the first, that he wanted to marry me…'but it is not yet time,' he would always say. I thought that the baby might help to make it 'time.'

"But instead, he became very angry. He shouted at me, and hit me, and knocked me down, there beside the pool. My head struck the floor, and I do not remember what happened after that, until I woke in a hospital.

"Richard did not come to visit me. I was not seriously hurt, and they released me the next day. But when I called, he would not speak to me. He threatened to go to the police, to tell them that I was a prostitute and a thief, and crazy, if ever I tried to see him again."

"People like that should be horsewhipped!" And Nick grunted in agreement, nodding, his fists clenched.

"I would have liked to kill him…but all that I had of him now was the baby. So I asked a friend to ask others what I should do. I bought medicines in three different stores, so they would not know what I was planning. And one night, I took them all together…"

"To cause a miscarriage?"

"Yes. My baby had never lived…but I killed it anyway."

I remembered a recent tragedy in my own life. "Suzanne, that happens sometimes even without drugs. A friend of mine back home slipped on the ice last winter, on the sidewalk, and lost her baby. The week before Christmas."

"Was it on purpose…or an accident?"

"An accident. She really wanted to have it."

"That is the difference, Jack, and the sin. I poisoned my baby on purpose: in hatred of Richard, and for revenge. Already I had broken the Sixth Commandment with him…and now I had broken the Fourth and Fifth also, by killing my own child."

"But couldn't you go to confession, and be forgiven? By a Catholic priest?"

"No. I simply could not face it. What if forgiveness were refused, or the penance made impossible for me? So I delayed, and delayed, until at last I decided there was no hope.

"Then I began, late at night, to hear a baby crying far away. Perhaps it was in another apartment, or perhaps I merely dreamed that I was awake and hearing it. But it sounded like the little lost spirit of my own baby, crying for the mother who had killed it.

"All of Paris, now, seemed a reminder of my guilt, so I resolved to leave. But surely I could not go home again to Mortagne, to my family. My parents would never accept what I had done. Then, tucked into a book of family pictures, I found an old letter from my Great-Aunt Clarisse, with her address. Possibly God the Mother guided me to find it then, when I most needed it.

"Clarisse had met an American soldier after World War Two, and they had fallen in love. He had not been a Catholic, so she had had to choose between him and the Church...and she had married him, and left Mortagne, and gone with him to America. To the Church, that is a mortal sin.

"My parents had always spoken of Clarisse with sorrow, as a lost soul. But I, too, was a lost soul now, and I decided to take what money I had saved and go to join her. Perhaps she would take me in, and at least we could be lost together.

"So I wrote to her, telling all which had happened...and she wrote back, and almost begged me to come, for her husband had died and she was all alone. So I came to America. And never, until today, have I told anyone else what really happened in Paris."

Alaine leaned forward and took both her hands.

"Suzanne, it wasn't your fault!"

"Yes, it was. I should never have gone with Richard."

"You said it yourself: he swept you off your feet. When that happens, you land on your back. It's a law of nature." She laughed, wryly. "Believe me, I know. Julian taught me. Right here!" and she slapped the rock beside her. "I just didn't get pregnant."

"Yes…and that makes a difference."

"How? Weren't you using any protection? Contraceptives? The Pill?"

"No. Those, too, are forbidden by the Church."

"So you're supposed to marry young, and spend your life raising little Catholics? Like your parents did?"

"Yes, that must be. But I did not…"

"Because Richard tricked you! Didn't he promise to marry you?"

"I thought that he had. But that night he said that I had only imagined it, or made it up: that he had never said it. Now, I do not know which is true."

"It doesn't matter. That kind of man, who'd throw you out on the street when you were pregnant with his child, would have lied to you anyway. He deceived you, and took advantage when you were drunk."

"I still killed my baby."

"What would have happened if you hadn't? Would

you have kept it, and tried to raise it by yourself? Or put it up for adoption?"

"I do not know. But now it would be alive. Not just a lost spirit crying in the night."

"Suzanne. Is that what you were talking about last week, on the way back from the Lair? Asking if I believed in ghosts?"

"Yes, Jack. Sometimes even now I wake late at night and think that I hear it. But I know that there is no baby in Charlie Blake's house, nor in any of the houses near it. So could it be only my imagination? Or is the ghost of my baby haunting me, even here?"

"I don't know. I didn't think I believed in ghosts. But until last week I didn't believe in fortune-telling, either. Or clairvoyance. Alaine, what do you think?"

"It's hard to say. Spirits of the dead do stay around sometimes, but seldom the ghosts of any so young. They never knew life, so they have no attachment to it. Ghosts are usually those who've lived a full life and don't want to stop. That, or there's a problem they still need resolved. Your abortion, Suzanne – if that's even what it was! – is your problem, not your baby's."

"Still, I took an innocent life. From hatred of Richard, I killed one who had done nothing to me."

"Maybe that baby wasn't ever meant to be born."

"What do you mean?"

"Maybe it was just a messenger."

"A messenger? From God?"

"Yes. Sent to show you what Richard really was. To pull off his mask. And then, when its work was done, to go back to Heaven again."

"But I still killed it…"

"Did you? Or would it have gone all by itself, when it had done its job? Would you have slipped on the ice or something, even without wanting to? Or had you lost it already, when Richard beat you up? Before you even took the medicine?"

"That, I do not know. Perhaps you are right."

"Suzanne, there's a line from another poem I think you should know. 'That which was never born can never die.' What goes up must come down, but you can't fall off a hill you never climbed. So think of it this way: you didn't kill your baby at all. You kept it from dying. By keeping it from being born."

"But it had been conceived. It was alive!"

"How do you know? Did you take a pregnancy test?"

"No. It was only that, for two months, I…I did not bleed."

"There are a lot of other things that can cause that, too. Stress, for instance. The stress of guilt, knowing that you'd let him seduce you…"

"But I was so certain that I was pregnant!"

"Did you even see a doctor – before that night in the

hospital? Did you ask about it, even then?"

"No. I would have been ashamed. I would have had to say that I was not married."

"Then there's no way to know, is there? You don't know you killed your baby, because you don't know there even was a baby. And even if there was, it may have been a messenger to save you from a situation God didn't want you in. Being the mistress of a jerk like Richard."

"But there was still the intent…"

"Suzanne, lots of people get mad and do things they regret later."

"Yes. But how many of them kill their babies?"

"Unborn babies? I'll bet it happens a lot more often than you think.

"Suzanne, I forgive you, and I think the Gods forgive you. I even think your baby forgives you. But it's obvious to me that **you** haven't forgiven you…and it won't be easy.

"I think, in a case like this, a Catholic priest would assign penance. Is that right?"

"Yes. I would be given some task to do, helping the poor or the sick, and many prayers to say. A great many prayers! Then, perhaps, I could be forgiven."

"Hmmm." Alaine pondered for a moment. "I don't have any experience doing this. I've never assigned penance before…" And then she was silent, for a long time.

Nick finally broke the silence. "Maybe you should ask the cards."

"Good idea. I'll have to leave the Circle to get them... Wait here. I'll be back."

Alaine rose and stepped to the Circle's rim, between the markers of the East and the North. With the tip of the white wand, then, she made a curious gesture: tracing a vertical line from above her head down to the rock at her feet, then raising her hands and moving them apart as if pushing aside some invisible curtain. Stepping forward through it, she walked halfway around the outside of the Circle, clockwise, to the South where our clothes lay.

Rummaging there she found her discarded jeans and dug a cloth-wrapped bundle from one of the pockets. Then still moving clockwise she returned to re-enter at the same point, then turned and redrew the vertical line, this time from the stone back upward. "Got them."

"Why did you do all that? Why not go right to where they were?"

"Because of the Circle. It's really there, you know. Not just something we imagine...even though our thoughts helped build it. I can see it sometimes, especially at night. It looks like a wall of faint sparkles, like a TV screen tuned to a blank channel. And I feel a sort of tingle if I touch it, as if the air there were full of electricity."

"I'll accept that, for now. But still, why the business with the wand? And why 'way over there, so far from the cards?"

"Because the Circle is cast from the East around to the North, there's a seam left; some call it the 'Way Between Worlds.' If you need to cross the Circle while it's set up, you should always do it there. Crossing it anywhere else, from the inside, could burst it like a bubble. And the gesture with the wand was the Opening of the Way."

"It looked like you were pulling down a zipper. Then pulling it up again, after you came back in."

"You know, Jack, that's a pretty good analogy. I visualize it more as cutting a slit in a curtain, and then 'un-cutting' it again. But your image is just as good, and it's something familiar to most people."

"Thanks. Maybe someday I'll learn to do it myself."

She smiled. "If the Moon Path leads you that way, I'll teach you." Sitting back down then, she unwrapped the cards from the knotted kerchief which held them. "Suzanne, would you shuffle these? I think it's time to do that reading you asked for last week."

"Yes." She took them and shuffled, rather clumsily. "I am sorry; this may take a long time. I am not used to handling cards."

"Take your time. We've got all afternoon!"

"When am I supposed to stop?"

"That's up to you. When I shuffle them I know by a tingly feeling I get in my hands: as if they'd partly gone to sleep. But for you, it may be something completely different."

Suzanne shuffled on, and on...and stopped at last. "My hands do not tingle, but they feel suddenly very tired. Does that mean that it is time?"

"I guess so. You stopped, didn't you?"

"Yes. So, here they are." And pushing the cards together, she gave them back to Alaine.

The priestess took and held them for a moment, eyes closed. "The question, then, is...what course should you take, to make amends for your sin?"

"Yes."

"Very well." Bending forward, Alaine laid out two cards side by side. "The inner forces: the Nine of Swords...and Justice. Sorrow and guilt for the loss of a loved one: Richard, or your baby. Probably both. And the need to pay whatever you owe, and restore balance to your life.

"So far, so good. Nothing we didn't already know, but it's a good reading when the first two cards confirm it so well.

"Now, the outer forces." She laid down four more cards surrounding the first two.

"The Five of Cups: loss, but not total. The Eight of Pentacles: learning through experience; the growth of skill and knowledge. That card shows up a lot in readings for students.

"The Hierophant: in Aunt Theda's deck, the Marseilles one, it was called the Pope. It represents organized religion, especially the outer forms, the dogmas. Things priests created to keep people coming to church, and money coming into the collection plates. The thousand laws of the Church, as opposed to the One Law of Love.

"And this one, the High Priestess, is the other side of religion, the side you don't see in a church. The inner doctrine, as opposed to the outer. I like to think it represents the Old Religion, as opposed to the New. It shows Suzanne now knows both sides and can choose which one she'll follow."

"So far, it's right on the money."

"Yes…so far. Now the vertical column: the answer to the question. What should she do to restore the balance? These will probably be in chronological order…"

Suzanne stared at the next card. "What? I should go out and hang myself?"

"No, not physically. The Hanged Man means a reversal of attitudes. Giving up the material for the spiritual, or the outer forms for the inner. It goes along with what we just saw: the Pope, and then the High Priestess."

She laid another card above it. "The Eight of Cups. Abandoning some project and starting another, often more difficult. Like the card of the Moon, it shows the way leading among mountains, by moonlight…"

"Are the cards saying that I am to take the same journey as Jack? And if so…. Alaine, will you be my guide also?"

"If I can. But remember, I don't know the way either."

Gesturing at the cards, Suzanne smiled. "No. But you can read the map better than I!"

"All right; I'll do what I can. Let's see what the next card says…"

"Death!"

"Relax! It's like the Hanged Man: not as bad as it looks. 'Death' is another card of change: destruction, but followed by renewal. Whatever is lost, will be replaced by something better. See, on the horizon: the two towers from The Moon. But here the Sun is rising between them."

"It still frightens me. But perhaps not as much, now. So what is the last card: the final outcome?"

Alaine turned it up and laid it at the end of the line. Her voice held dismay. "The Eight of Swords?"

I bent forward and studied it. The card showed a

figure standing bound and blindfolded, surrounded by swords thrust into the ground, upright like prison bars. "What does it mean?"

"Inability to resolve a situation without help. Waste of energy in useless action. Making plans that come to nothing. But what can it mean here? All the cards showing change, renewal, a journey toward higher things. Then, this?"

"Could it mean she needs to get a certain distance on her own, then wait for help from somebody else?"

"It could. I don't understand it. She starts out on the journey just fine, makes some major breakthrough…and then, just stops. Unless…"

Slowly then she began to nod. "Yes, it could…."

" 'Yes'? What could be?"

"Maybe, Suzanne, those last two cards don't refer to you personally at all."

"Then to whom?"

"Suppose we take the 'Death' card literally. Maybe these cards are talking about somebody else. Somebody who's already passed through the Gate, and is stuck for some reason on the other side." Alaine's finger tapped the figure in the Eight of Swords.

"The ghost of my baby! I am somehow to help it, then, escape from Limbo? But how?"

"I don't know. You need to take the Moon Path, though, to find it. I'm sure of that much, and I'll help all I can. But the rest, we'll have to figure out as we go."

"Then I will do it. And that will be a part of my penance. But should there not be more, also?"

"Prayers?"

"Yes. A priest would have assigned a task, as you have…but also, a great many prayers. For my lesser sins, I would usually say ten, or twenty, or fifty *Ave Marias*. But for this, I feel, many hundreds would be needed."

"That sounds like a teacher making you write 'I will not talk in class' a hundred times on the board after school. You should say the prayer, of course, but it shouldn't be just a punishment. Prayer should never be a punishment! It should help you get back in tune with God, or the Gods…by whatever Names you call Them."

"Let me think…" Alaine stared off past us for a moment, then began to nod. "Yes. I have a…sort of notebook back in my room, that I've copied things into through the years. Things Aunt Theda taught me, and things I found in books, and some that I've written myself. Let me go through it, and copy out some passages for you. Prayers to the Goddess, and maybe the Charge…"

"Prayers for me to say, to God the Mother?"

"If you feel comfortable with them, yes. I'll get those to you sometime next week. You already know the Goddess from the Pope's side, as Holy Mary. Now, it's time you learned to see Her from the High Priestess' side. Without Her mask!"

"But should I not say my *Ave Marias*, also?"

"I don't know how those go, but if they've helped you before I'm sure they'll help now. And they are prayers to the Goddess, aren't they?"

"In a way. Perhaps I should say one here and now: for Her, and for you also, so that you will know what it is. These are the words of the Angel Gabriel, when He came to Mary and told Her that She was to be the mother of Jesus. I learned them in Latin…but I will translate them into English as I say them."

Suzanne knelt upright on the stone, hands clasped and head bowed. "Hail, Mary, grace-filled; God is with You. Blesséd are You of women…and blesséd the fruit of your belly, Jesus." Her voice was growing ragged with emotion as she spoke. "Holy Mary, Mother of God…pray for us, who are sinners…" Choking up, she could go no further.

I rose then, and knelt beside her, taking her hand. "Suzanne, it's all right. Is there more?"

Her eyes were squeezed tightly shut, and tears were leaking out as she nodded. "But I…cannot."

"Why?"

"I…I am not worthy."

"Who is, really? But this is the best we can do: keep

on asking for God's help, so maybe, finally, we can become worthy. At least that's what my church taught, back before I left it. Didn't yours?"

"Yes, I suppose so… Jack, will you pray it with me?"

"You'll have to teach me the words. I can repeat it after you if you like."

"Please." Gripping my hand very hard, she started again midway. "Holy Mary, Mother of God… Pray for us, who are sinners…now, and in the hour of our death… Amen."

I repeated the words with her. "Amen."

With that final word her tears burst forth. I put my arm around her, and sobbing she buried her face in my shoulder. Gently I held her then, rocked her and rubbed her shoulders until at last the flow subsided. Sue clung to me in silence for a few minutes more, then gently pulled away. "Thank you, Jack. I am all right now."

"Is there anything else I can do?"

"No. Nothing." She sat back down on the rock. "Alaine, I think that I will be able to say them now. How many?"

"Whatever you think is best. How many would a priest have assigned?"

"For a small, common sin, ten or twenty. But for me…" She shook her head.

"Then why don't you let the Goddess set the

number? Say…five each night, until She shows you what the rest of your penance is to be."

"Yes. I will, every night before I sleep."

"And when I've given you those other prayers, you might add in one or two of them. Ones you particularly like, or feel comfortable with."

"I will. And then perhaps She will listen to me, and show me what else I must do to be forgiven."

"Good. I guess we're finished with the Circle, then, except for the Cakes and Wine…"

"What are those?"

"Sacraments of the Old Religion. Probably the ancestors of the Bread and Wine at the Last Supper."

Suzanne's eyes widened. "The Mass?"

"Nothing so formal. Just a symbolic meal, shared with each other and with the Gods. Almost every religion has it, in one form or another."

"But it is the Body and Blood of Christ!"

"A symbol can have different meanings to different people. For us, it represents the gifts of the Gods. Bread to sustain our own bodies, and wine to lift our spirits!"

"All right. Alaine, I see that if I am to follow this path, there are many things which I must learn…and un-learn. But am I worthy to receive your Sacraments? I am not even a member of your religion."

"You've come into this Church. You've confessed

The Moon Path

what happened in Paris. You've been forgiven, as much as I can forgive you myself without the Lady's intervention. You've had penance assigned, as much as we can for now, and you've already done part of it. What more do you need?"

"Nothing, I suppose. If you say that it is all right?"

"It's all right, Suzanne. You're welcome to. And I'd like you to."

"Then I will. Nick, would you help?"

"Sure. But don't we need a cup for the wine? And your *athamé*?"

"We'll pass the bottle instead. For now just hold it in one hand, and the 'cakes' in the other.... Good. And again the wand will do instead." She stood and raised it high in both hands, point-upward like a lightning rod, as Nick knelt before her with the bottle and the little package of Melba toast she'd handed him.

"O Queen of Moon and Stars, bless this food and drink. Let it grant health and strength to our bodies; joy and peace to our minds; and to our spirits, that fulfillment of love which brings eternal happiness." She traced the five-pointed star with the tip of the wand, then brought it smoothly down to touch the uppermost piece of toast in Nick's hand. "So mote it be."

We echoed, "So mote it be."

Nick handed her the bottle. "Blesséd be." Taking a

Jack Peredur
141

long drink from it, she passed it on to me. "Blessèd be."

The wine had warmed, but it was still delicious. After drinking deeply I passed it to Suzanne, repeating the formula: "Blessèd be."

She drank, and Nick took the bottle and set it down. Alaine took the four slices of Melba toast from him and gave one to each of us, again with the same words: "Blessèd be."

There was silence for a moment then, save for the crunching of teeth. Nick was the first to speak again. "Alaine, that was good. But when do we eat? This was just enough to tell me I'm starving!"

"In time, Nick. Does anyone else have anything to do or say before we open the Circle?"

"Alaine...I want to thank you again, and to thank...the Goddess, also. For almost a year, I have been in despair: thinking that I dared not face God. But now I know it was only the priests and their Church which I dared not face. And here, in God's place, I think God – and Goddess! – have heard me after all."

"Then, Suzanne, welcome again to the Circle. And blessèd be!"

Fresh tears were on her face, but through them Suzanne was smiling. "Blessèd be, Alaine."

In the same order in which Alaine had summoned the Elemental Guardians, she now dismissed them. "...Keeper of the Powers of Earth: we thank You for

Your presence and protection. Depart now, with our blessings…and come again, when next we call upon You." The wand-tip moved again, tracing the five-pointed star…but this one began and ended at one of the lower points.

"Eternal Gods! Father and Mother of All: we thank You for Your presence here, and pray that You will remain with us even as we leave this holy Circle." The wand traced again the star of six points above us. "So mote it be!"

And we echoed once more, "So mote it be!"

Stepping then to the northeast, she raised the wand as before and cut downward through the Circle's wall. This time, her stroke did not end when wand-tip touched stone but cut inward across the line she'd traced earlier. As she did I felt something odd, a little like the sudden change of air pressure when a door is opened in a windowless room: felt it not in my ears, but somewhere in my mind. And suddenly I noticed the rustle of leaves above us, and the singing of birds, as if the invisible wall had somehow shut those sounds away.

"The Circle is open, but never broken," Alaine announced. "Those within it now return from the place of the Gods, back to the mortal world. In joy we met; in joy, then, let us part. Blesséd be!"

"Blesséd be!"

Going to fetch back the towels, the food and drinks into the opened Circle, I'd thought of bringing in my clothes too. As I walked, though, twinges of pain recalled another day to me: the day of that ill-fated hike as a Pioneer Boy in August of '62.

We'd gone five miles through the summer heat, from our camp near Goshen Pond to a secluded swimming hole further down the Mullica River. With our Trailblazer's tacit permission some troop members had gone in naked, but bashful, blanket-grabbing Jack had worn trunks and kept them on, still damp, under the Pioneer uniform for the hike back afterward. A mistake! By the time we'd made our way back to camp I'd been in agony from inner thighs chafed raw, gritting my teeth lest I show signs of it and the others make fun of me.

The boys might not have noticed I was hurting, but our Trailblazer did. Taking me aside once we'd arrived, with a shaking head he'd checked the damage. "Whoa. That must hurt. A lot!"

Biting my lip, I'd silently nodded.

"Never, ever hike in wet clothes. Especially wet underwear! The *Pioneer Handbook's* clear on that. And now you know why. And why I didn't say anything when those others went in trunkless."

Rummaging through the troop's first-aid kit then, he'd come up with a little yellow tube and pressed it into my hand. "This should help." *PICROTINE*, the label had read.

"Wash those well," he'd told me. "Blot them dry, then spread on some of this. It'll ease the pain and help them heal.

"And lose those trunks, so they don't just wipe it off again! Just 'go Scottish' these next few days…" and with a chuckle, he'd explained about Highland kilts and what Scotsmen normally wore under them. "It's no disrespect to the uniform to go bare underneath, if it helps you heal!"

The stuff from the tube had been gooey, but immediately soothing. Too bad I didn't have any here at the quarry! "Going Scottish," though, seemed like a world-class idea just now, even *sans* kilt or uniform.

Leaving my clothes where they lay, I went back bare to join the others.

Spreading out the food at center and the towels around it, we sat down and ate. The rest of the afternoon we spent mostly there, on the stone or in the water. It was clear nobody else wanted to get dressed again either: "not while it's so warm, and there's nobody else here!"

"Yes. That would be a shame, to put our 'masks' back on so soon!"

"It'd be another shame, though, to go back Monday with all-over sunburn!"

"Then I will simply stay here under the trees until it is time to go." And shaking the crumbs off her towel Suzanne spread it out on the stone and lay face-down on it: one arm under her head as a pillow, and her face turned toward us. "After all of the food, and the wine, I may even go to sleep. Would anyone mind?"

"No, of course not. We might as well do the same thing…"

So we cleared away the litter of the meal, and shook out our own towels, and spread them. "May I join you?"

"Yes, Jack. I would like that."

I lay down then on my side facing her, with Alaine and Nick behind me. She smiled, and I reached out to stroke her hair again. For a minute or so, she let me…but then her other hand came up and took mine, and firmly set it back on the stone between us.

"What's the matter?"

Her fingers squeezed mine. "Jack, I like it when you do that. But without clothes, it makes me think that perhaps you will want to touch me in other ways, also. And that cannot be."

She was right about my stray thoughts. It had been a long time since those nights with Judith at Rutgers! "Why not?"

"Because that was the start of my trouble with Richard. I like you very much, but I am not ready to begin thinking of making love again. I am sorry."

Now I felt like a fool. "I'm sorry too. I should have understood…"

"You wanted to comfort me, I know. And it is all right. We are friends, and I am comfortable with you. I trust you, and I can take off my mask with you. But I am not ready for anything more."

"Sure. Sorry if I came on too strong."

"You did not. And there is nothing for which to be sorry." Drawing my hand toward her face she kissed the back of it lightly. "I trust you, Jack, and I want you near. But for now, at least, only as a friend."

"Sure." Taking her own hand, I kissed it in return. "As a friend."

So I turned on my back, and we lay there side by side on the warm stone, hand in hand…and slept.

9 Toads

May 22, 1971

It was late afternoon when Nick woke us. Tree-shadows reached halfway up the quarry's far walls. "Better wake up. Unless you want to walk home in the dark."

"What time is it?"

"Five-thirty. We've got about two hours 'til sunset."

Jack Peredur

"Okay. Suzanne? Are you awake?"

"I am now. But, oh, Jack, I was having such a beautiful dream!"

"What was it?"

"It started in Mortagne. I was going to church, wearing my best clothes and shoes, as I did every Sunday and holy day when I was young. The church was full of people, as usual. Strangely, though, the altar was missing. There was a door now in the wall, beyond where it had been. As I walked up the aisle, the door slowly opened and I knew that I must go through it.

"Beyond it was dark, and the door closed behind me with a terrible boom, as if it would never open again. I was alone in the darkness, and at first I was afraid: afraid that the church had cast me out forever, into the darkness of Hell. But then I saw moonlight, and it showed me that I had actually come into a second church: shaped like the first, but outdoors and much larger, with rows of huge old trees making its walls. The vault overhead was the net of their branches, with the full moon shining through. It was very beautiful. A church of Nature!

"But its altar, too, was missing. Instead, the front of the church was simply open. It looked out across a lake, at the same scene which is on Alaine's card of the Moon. The moonlight shone on the water, and beyond I could see the road leading up between the towers.

The Moon Path

"There was another light, also, on that far shore. Jack, it was you: standing like the Hermit on that other card, holding up your lamp to light my way. Except it was a chemistry flask, I think, full of something glowing green.

"And behind you were Alaine and Nick, and others whom I could not recognize: all waiting there at the start of the road, and beckoning, and calling to me. And I wanted very much to be with you, to walk with you wherever that road might lead us.

"I took off my shoes and began to wade across. But it quickly grew too deep, and in my 'Sunday best' clothes I could not swim. So I took them off also and let them sink, or float away behind me. And in 'God's best' I swam across, to join you all on the Moon Path. I was just beginning to climb out again when you woke me."

Kneeling, Alaine took her hand. "I think you've already joined us, Suzanne. Do you understand the dream?"

"Yes, I think so.

"I passed through the Christian church, and then out into darkness. That is my past, at home and then with Richard. The door closed, shutting me out of that church, and I thought that I would wander in the darkness forever. That is where I was when I came to America. But then the Moon appeared and showed me that all of the world is a church, and better than the one which I left.

"Alaine, are you the Moon?"

"No. I'm just a guide. Remember?"

"Yes: the Hermit. And my dream seems to say Jack will be another, so we will be walking in the light of the old ways and the new, blended in harmony.

"But then who is the Moon? The Goddess?"

Alaine smiled. "The Moon is one of Her symbols. Maybe the oldest of all.

"One of the things Aunt Theda left me was a headband with a silver crescent on it: the crown of a High Priestess. She'd never worn it in this country because she'd always worshipped alone here, or with me. But I think she hoped someday I could form a coven of my own, and hold the old Sabbath rites, and earn the right to wear it myself."

A chill ran suddenly up my back. "A **coven?** But doesn't that mean a group of **witches**?"

At my mention of the word, Suzanne paled; she drew her hand from Alaine's and crossed herself, her lips moving in some silent prayer. Alaine turned to me. I'd expected her to be angry, but she was not. "What are witches, Jack?"

"Fairy-tale women who make poison brews? And worship the Devil? And turn people into toads?"

"Do you believe that?"

"No. But if not that, then what?"

"How about priestesses…and priests, too…of a religion much older than Christianity?"

I was beginning to understand. "Priests and priestesses who lay out cards to see the future. And worship the God and Goddess outdoors, naked, in a Circle. And share cakes and wine afterward?"

She nodded, smiling. "When they can."

"But why the toads, then? And the Devil?"

"If you were the Christian church, trying to keep your people away from the Old Religion – the witches – what would you tell them?"

"That witches served the Devil, and had strange, evil powers. Like cooking up poison. Or turning Christians into toads!"

"See? The most successful smear campaign in history! And that, Suzanne, is why the High Priestess wears a mask. And why not all 'Gypsies' are *Romni*!"

"Then **you** are a witch. And your Aunt Theda, and the 'Gypsies' who taught her. And you want me to be one, also?"

"If you want to be. It's your own choice. Nobody will force you. But would you rather go back and try to be a Christian again?"

Suzanne was silent for a long time, but when she spoke again her voice was resolute. "No. That door closed behind me, and it will never open again. I must go forward now, toward the moonlight. Toward the Goddess.

"Already I have cast off my Sunday clothes. I have taken off my mask to you, and confessed my sins as if to a Christian priest, and you have forgiven me. Now you are calling to me from the Moon Path, and I want to join you, no matter what evil name others may have given you. For I do not think that you are evil, nor an agent of evil.

"Perhaps I am wrong. Perhaps it is all a trick, and the Devil is laughing. But if that is true, then my soul is lost already, because of my baby. You have given me hope. And I know no other path, now, which I might follow.

"So I will step forward onto the Moon Path…or swim forward to it, as in my dream. If I sink and fall into Hell? Well, that is a chance which I have already taken. But I believe now that the water will hold me up, and that the Goddess waits for me somewhere ahead."

She reached up to unfasten the chain of her medal, took it off, gave the figure on it one long last look, kissed it, then laid it gently on the stone beside her and took both of Alaine's hands in hers. "I do not know what more I must do…but I am ready. If you, and the Goddess, will help me…I will be a witch."

Alaine hugged her, and her voice was husky with

emotion. "Then welcome, Suzanne! Welcome. From me, and from Her."

And Nick came forward to embrace them both in his huge dark arms. "Glad you're here, Suzanne. Blesséd be!"

"Are you, also, a witch?"

"A Novice: the same as you are, now. Alaine's been teaching me for a couple of months."

"Then I feel less alone. And I am glad that you will be with me."

She turned to me, then. "Jack, what about you?"

"I don't know. I guess I'm sort of a Methodist, but not a very good one. Alaine, is it possible to be both? A witch, and a Christian?"

She pondered. "Up to a point, I guess. I never really thought about it. Are you interested?"

"I don't know. I like a lot of the things you've told us. I like the idea of using natural places as churches. And I think I could get used to not wearing clothes. Maybe I already have. It's certainly more comfortable in all this heat." I smiled. "And I can't complain about the view, either!

"But Suzanne's already used to a female deity, from praying to Holy Mary. We never had that where I came from."

"I understand that. You were brought up on the straight Trinity doctrine, weren't you?"

"Yes. And the Ten Commandments, and the Sermon on the Mount…"

"What's the most important thing your religion tells you to do?"

I pondered. "I guess it's to let our lives be ruled by love. Christ Himself told us, 'Love the Lord thy God with all thy heart, and soul, and mind, and strength. And love thy neighbor as thyself.'"

"Christ was a great teacher, though we don't consider Him a God. Witches live by the same Law He taught: the Law of Love. We just express it a little differently.

"I already quoted one form of it, what Aunt Theda called the Wiccan Rede: 'An ye hurt none, do as ye will!' You could call that our 'Golden Rule', I guess. But there's a much deeper statement of it, in what we call the 'Charge of the Goddess':

"To serve Me strive always for love, and for love alone. All else will follow, for all acts of love and pleasure are My rituals. Sacrifice neither gold nor blood, for both are naught to Me. Share with Me instead your joy, for I am with you and within you always. Worship Me in all you do, through honor and humility, reverence, love and compassion for all things living.

"For Mine is the joy of the spirit, and joy on Earth as well. And My only Law is Love."

"Alaine, that was beautiful! And that's what witches believe?"

She nodded. "I learned it from Aunt Theda. But I've found the same thing, almost word-for-word, in several different books. Is that good enough?"

"What more could I ask?"

"A lot, Jack, if you wanted to. And I'm sure you will.

"You're welcome to study the materials I'll be giving Suzanne. In fact, I recommend you work on them together. And you don't have to decide right away. Take your time, and learn everything you can. I don't want anybody coming into my coven who isn't completely comfortable with the teachings.

"You're both welcome to find me, or Nick, and ask any questions you may have. The worst we'll do is tell you it's stuff we need to be in Circle to discuss. And when we can, we'll do that too."

"Why don't we plan to come back here, then...a week from today?"

"Fine. We can meet in the lobby again. And if it's raining, we'll go up to my room instead."

"Is that legal? At Rutgers, men weren't allowed past the lobby in the women's dorms."

"We're a little better off here. One of us has to be with you, and they'll make a fuss if you try to stay past ten on a weeknight. But on weekends you can come up any time you like: the same as in the men's dorms."

"I didn't know that. We'll plan on it, then. All right with you, Suzanne? Nick?"

"Certainly."

"Sure. But we'd better pack up now and move on. I just heard a mosquito go by. And none of us brought repellant." He gestured around at the four of us. "Must think it's in mosquito heaven!"

"I guess you're right, Nick." Picking up her brassiere, Alaine gave it a disgusted look. "Time to put the masks back on..."

Dressed again – though I went "Scottish" now under my jeans, torn trunks exiled to the bundled towel I carried! – we headed back to campus. The sun was setting as we neared the Student Union beach, the water empty and silent now, but the lights were still on in the snack bar facing it. "Who else wants a burger? I'm starved!"

"Nick, you're always starved! But I could use one too."

Double glass doors opened to a canteen, a smaller sibling to the one in the main Student Union. It was crowded, loud with jukeboxes and pinball machines, but the food was palatable. My appetite surprised me, and I polished off a double cheeseburger and two orders of fries.

Nick and Alaine kept up a running conversation

while we ate. They discussed classes, and approaching tests, and a minor problem with Nick's motorcycle, just as if our day had held nothing out of the ordinary. I half-listened in growing frustration. So much had happened today: so much which I, at least, had felt was important. How could they now be going on and on this way about such trivia?

And the students at the next table over were just adding to my irritation, with their increasingly loud discussion about what the country should, or should not, be doing in Viet Nam. Why couldn't they keep their stupid political opinions to themselves?

Then, of course, it hit me: if we could hear them so easily, then anyone at the tables nearby could also hear us. So Nick and Alaine were simply creating another form of camouflage, another mask for us all: a mask of words, in case others might overhear. And Suzanne and I, sitting in silent awe at the vistas the day had opened to us, weren't helping.

My irritation vanished. Some witch I'd make! I tried, then, to take part in the conversation. But my heart wasn't in it, and whatever I said sounded inane to me. After today's revelations, it was just too hard to concentrate on the trivia of daily life. Soon I returned to silence.

Even when the food was gone and Nick and Alaine had left us, Suzanne and I found few words to say even to each other: as if what had happened at the quarry were too special, too sacred to be discussed anywhere else. We walked the remaining mile to Charlie Blake's house almost without conversation. But Suzanne held my hand tightly all the way...and she didn't pull away when I embraced her gently on the doorstep. In my ear, she whispered, "Blesséd be."

"You're really sure you want to join, aren't you?"

"Yes. I must! And I would love to have you study with me, and join when I do. But if you decide that you will not? I promise that I will not turn you into a toad."

"Thanks. I can't promise I'll join: not until I've learned a lot more. But I know I felt more at home in Alaine's Circle today, and closer to God, than I ever did in church growing up."

"Perhaps there is no one true religion. Someone once said that all religions are ways of looking at the same truths, through windows which the priests have painted with different colors.

"If so, I very much like the view through Alaine's window!"

"So do I. Suzanne..."

"Yes?"

"Blesséd be."

She smiled. "Blesséd be, Jack." And kissing me lightly on the cheek, she pulled free of my arms and went inside.

10 Burning

May 23, 1971

Sunday morning, I woke up in Hell.

At least I thought so for a moment, immersed in heat and pain and the fragments of terrible dreams. It wasn't the world around me, though, that was burning. It was me.

My top sheet lay crumpled at the foot of the bed, where I must have kicked it in my sleep; the bottom sheet was soaked with sweat. My thighs, my stomach, my chest, my upper arms, all shone bright red in the morning light. Pushing down the waistband of my shorts, I saw the color continued without a break.

My shoulders, back, and buttocks were the worst, crimson in the mirror; they felt as if someone had ironed them. My ears, nose, and forehead were almost as bad. I hadn't been this burned since a summer in my teens, after a long day shirtless at the beach. A numbing ointment from a drug store had helped a lot, but I hadn't seen Burn-Zo-Caine in years; like Picrotine, it seemed to have vanished from the shelves.

Aspirin, though, was always my best friend when my back gave me trouble. Might it help here too? Finding a near-empty bottle in the medicine cabinet, I gulped down four tablets. As always, they tasted terrible.

Remembering how pinkly pale Suzanne had been, I guessed she might be in even worse shape today…and wondered how she might explain her condition to Charlie Blake.

Clearly, we'd overstayed our welcome in the sun. We'd be spending today, and much of the week to come, paying for that!

I considered staying in the room all day, turning the air conditioner to maximum and trying to sleep through the worst of it. But I'd gotten out of working in the

Holy of Holies on Saturday only by promising to spend today there, preparing materials for Doctor Knight's research. The weekend's load of studying was waiting for me, too.

Well, Stanford Hall had its own air conditioning, usually set a little cooler than it needed to be for comfort. Once or twice during the past week I'd almost wished for a sweater, or at least long sleeves. Now, though, the chill might work to my advantage. So I dressed: covering the thigh chafe with a jumbo Band-Aid, then putting on my lightest shirt and my oldest, softest jeans before going on over.

The day passed in varying degrees of discomfort. Doctor Knight himself was out of town and would be until Wednesday, presenting a paper at a conference in Philadelphia. Few others had come in today, so at least I was able to work and suffer undisturbed by any visitors.

I had one companion, though, all day. Before leaving my mentor had set up a maze of glass plumbing, holding at its center a paper filter with crumbled dry leaves from a packet marked "Passion Vine (*Passiflora incarnata*)." Marked pages in a book from his office explained what it was: a Soxhlet extractor, in which a boiling solvent – toluene, in this case – would condense, drip through the leaves and leach out anything soluble into the flask below. A chemist's equivalent, in other words, of an ordinary coffee percolator. Of course, he wanted me to run it for him while he was away, several batches if I could, and had left additional notes explaining how.

Starting the extractor took almost half an hour of constant attention: I had to increase the heat and the water flow alternately, little by little, to reach full capacity without a boilover. But after that, it needed just an occasional check and trifling adjustment to keep it running smoothly. In relief I laid aside those cumbersome safety goggles – *just another mask to wear*, I thought, *working for Doctor Knight*! – and started on my homework while the Soxhlet bubbled and gurgled.

To avoid the midday heat, and the problems of stopping and restarting the temperamental extractor, I got my lunch from the vending machines in the Student Lounge: some peanut-butter crackers, a Pluto Pie, and a Coke to wash down the last of the aspirin from my bottle in the room. Though we weren't supposed to have food in the laboratories and Doctor Knight had already scolded me for bringing drinks there, since I'd be alone today I made an exception and ate at my desk.

That Coke, and another one later, saw me through to eight o'clock. I'd caught up by then on my coursework, and read ahead in the textbooks. The liquid dripping from the extractor was clear now, while that in the boiling flask was dark brown. Deciding Doctor Knight's "coffee" was probably ready I turned off the heater, leaving the condenser running to trap any stray vapor still in the system and send it down one last time through the leaves. A second batch could wait for tomorrow!

The sun had set by the time I left Stanford Hall, though the outside air still seemed furnace-hot to me. I got a cold supper at the Student Union: a sandwich, a couple of boiled eggs and yet another Coke. Their little drugstore section was very basic – the clerk hadn't seen Picrotine in years, and had never even heard of Burn-Zo-Caine! – but at least there was plenty of aspirin. I took two on the spot, then went back to the dorm: planning to go to bed early, hoping the night would bring further healing.

Room 315 was full of black light again, Led Zeppelin on the stereo, as Hadrian studied by the glow of his candle. "Hey, there! Welcome back."

I grunted something ill-tempered, already peeling off my sweat-soaked clothes to crawl "Scottish" under the sheet. At least this room was cooler than the air outdoors. I'd really hoped to have it to myself, though, for however long it would take to fall asleep.

Alas, I couldn't find a position that didn't bring some degree of pain. With the sheet over me, I was too hot; without it the air conditioner's breeze felt like phantom insects crawling. Whatever part of my body touched the bed would soon itch unbearably, and I'd have to roll over again. That lingering chafe from the trunks was still bothering me, too....

It might have been an hour or more that I lay there in torment. Finally, Hadrian spoke again. "Could you be a little quieter? I can't concentrate, and this is due tomorrow."

"Sorry. I got too much sun yesterday, and I can't find a position that's comfortable."

"Sunburn? That can be bad, I know. Aspirin might help, or.... Hmmm!"

"Yeah?"

"Maybe...Jack, maybe I can help. Would you let me try something?"

"What?"

"Have you ever been hypnotized?"

"No, not that I remember. Why? Are you a hypnotist?"

"No. But maybe I can help you hypnotize yourself, just enough to relax and get to sleep."

I pondered. Hadrian might have some odd theories about the world, but that hypnosis book on his shelf had looked well-worn, well-studied. "What would I have to do?"

"Just lie there, on your back, the way you are now. Look at..." He studied the view through the window.

"Nothing there to focus on. Damn." He bent to rummage in his desk drawer.

Rising with something luminous in his hand, he stuck it high on the wall directly in front of me: a fluorescent sticker, one of those round yellow smiley-faces that had been everywhere a year or two before. "So, focus on that sticker. Take slow, deep breaths. And count, with each breath, backward from a hundred. Start now."

Mentally, I started the count. "One hundred… ninety-nine…ninety-eight…ninety-seven…"

Hadrian was still talking. "Keep counting. Even though you hear my voice, don't listen to it. Think of it as something in the background, like music on the radio, helping you relax…as you keep on counting…"

"…Ninety-four…ninety-three…ninety-two…"

"…Helping you relax, like background music, or the sound of waves on a seashore…"

"…Eighty-nine…eighty-eight…eighty-seven…"

"…And as you count, feel yourself growing more and more relaxed…my voice helping…"

"…Eighty-four…eighty-three…"

"…With every breath, your eyelids getting heavier…"

"…Seventy-six…seventy-five…"

"…So relaxed, so heavy, that soon they'll close by themselves…"

"...Seventy-two..."

"...Heavier and heavier...and now they're closing...just relax, and let it happen...taking slow, deep breaths...and counting..."

"...Sixty-eight..."

"...Deeper and deeper now, relaxed and tired, so tired..."

"...Sixty-three..."

"...Until it's too much effort even to count..."

"...Sixty-...one..."

"...Too much effort, because you're so relaxed, so tired..."

"...Sixty?..."

"...And when that happens, just relax still further because you don't have to count anymore. Just relax...so tired..."

"...Fifty-nine...fifty...fifty..."

"...Tired...relaxed...slowly, now, drifting away into sleep..."

"...Fifty..."

"...Drifting into a deep, deep sleep..."

"...Fif...ty...?"

"...Sleep..."

11 "Relax..."

May 24, 1971

The next thing I knew, it was morning. I'd not set the alarm clock, but it didn't matter. Since he'd be away today and tomorrow, Doctor Knight had settled for giving us extra homework in lieu of a lecture. It had kept me busy most of Sunday when I hadn't been tending the Soxhlet extractor, but I'd finished it.

So I woke up slowly, without help. The room didn't

seem as hot this morning, though it was well past nine and sunlight was streaming through the window. In the mirror I still looked like a half-boiled lobster, but the color had faded a little since yesterday and I wasn't quite as sore, either.

Hadrian, of course, was long gone.

Rummaging in the closet, I dug out a towel and the soft old cotton lab coat I'd brought from home to use as a lightweight bathrobe. With my spare key in a pocket and soap in hand I set out for the showers down the hall. As I'd hoped, they were empty: nobody there to ask me how I'd gotten this all-over sunburn. I turned on the water, blending it barely lukewarm to spare my stinging shoulders.

Feeling much better after fifteen or twenty minutes under the spray I returned to the room, shaved, and began to dress. Sunday's jeans, I decided, would do for another day. Sunday's shirt, though, was wrinkled and stank of sweat. Consigning it to the laundry basket I put on one not quite as well-worn, not quite as soft. Too bad I couldn't just wear that lab coat today, I thought, and go "Scottish" underneath!

By then, though, it was ten-thirty and I was hungry, so I dressed and walked down to the Student Union. Nick had recommended their ham-and-fried-egg sandwiches last week, so I decided to try one.

The place wasn't as crowded as I'd seen it last;

many tables were empty, and others had one or two people at them instead of the usual four. And at one in the back corner, as far as possible from the pinball machines and jukebox, sat Nick himself: waving to me with one hand, a double cheeseburger in the other, and a second burger sitting in front of him waiting its turn to be devoured.

Waving back I headed for the counter, a poppy-seed bagel with ham and cheese on my mind…only to learn they'd stopped preparing breakfast at ten. I bought a couple of pre-wrapped sausage biscuits instead, and coffee.

By the time I joined him, Nick was halfway through that second burger. "Have a seat."

"Thanks." Setting my biscuits on the table I sat down carefully, wincing a little. "I stayed out too long Saturday: forgot how easily I burn. Guess we need to take sun lotion next time. Did it get you too?"

"Not much." He grinned. "Must be my 'southern' blood."

"I wish I had more. My Mom's part Italian, but it's 'way back. And Dad's people were English and German, mostly."

"You'll just have to tan in easier stages." He took another big bite, chewed, swallowed. "Oh, Jack, I saw an ad you might be interested in."

"What kind of ad?"

"Tried to find that old combination lock, but I couldn't. So this morning I went by Thorson's Hardware: you know, across from the Lair in the next block down?"

"I hadn't noticed it. Good to know there's one around."

He nodded. "Practically grew up in one, didn't you?"

"I guess. I helped Dad out behind the counter a lot: that, and did odd jobs for customers. Painting, plumbing, a little carpentry..."

"Thought so. Right up your alley, then."

"What, the ad? Somebody wants their house remodeled? Nick, I don't have time for that anymore!"

"Might want to make time for this one."

"Why? Whose is it?"

"Could be yours."

"What do you mean?"

"Will Thorson used to sell lumber, too. Kept it in an old house back of the store. Ripped out the walls inside, except what it took to hold things up, and one room upstairs he used for an office. All the rest was lumber room. Kept the paint out there, too.

"Then Builder-Mart opened, out past Seven Oaks. Thorson couldn't beat their prices, so after a few years of fighting he joined them: gave up on lumber and sold them all they'd take of his stock, for about ten cents on the dollar."

"The same thing happened to my Dad. That's why I'm here where tuition is cheap, instead of still at Rutgers!"

He nodded. "Anyway… House has been empty for years now, except for the stuff Builder-Mart didn't want. Thorson won't sell, though: says real estate's the best investment there is. Wants to rent it out, make enough to pay the taxes. But who'd rent a place like that, just a shell?"

"Some fix-it-up nut, I guess. Why?"

"It's cheap, Jack. And it's close to campus. Thought you might be interested."

"Intrigued, maybe. How cheap is 'cheap'?"

"He was asking ninety a month, but nobody bit. So now he's offering just the top floor for fifty-five. You can remodel any way you want, as long as it meets code. Bottom floor's still full of junk, but he says anything there you can use, it's yours free."

"Fifty-five a month? For a semester, that would be two hundred-plus. The dorm only costs me one-eighty."

"For 'half a prison cell', I think you said. And a roommate breathing down your neck. This is the whole second floor in a good-sized house!"

"About to fall down, though, probably."

"I doubt it. Brick. Looks solid to me."

"Nick, it's an interesting idea…but no. What would I want with all that room? All I need is a place to sleep!"

"Just thought I'd mention it. You were so desperate last week to find a place off-campus for the fall."

"I still am. But not an empty warehouse!"

"All right…

"By the way: got a new lock while I was there, and some brown spray paint to make it 'old and rusty.' As soon as it's dry, I'll go put the chain back up."

"Good. Maybe then nobody else will find the place."

He nodded. "Might get to slow-tan your British hide after all."

"Right now, that doesn't appeal. I don't even want to think about the sun for a while! …How's Alaine?"

"A little pink around the edges, but not bad. That wasn't her first time out."

"Good. I'm worried about Suzanne, though. She must be fried!"

"Needs to take it a little at a time. Maybe you two should get a sun lamp."

"And use it at Charlie's? Both of us? Naked?" I shook my head. "He'd be shocked!"

"Not if you were living up behind Thorson's…"

"That again?"

"Just thought I'd mention it…"

"Why don't you rent it, then? It might be cheaper than your trailer."

"What? And have to move all my stuff?"

"You've only been here six months! How much 'stuff' have you got?"

"Six months? I lived in Belvedere all my life, and I've been going back 'most every weekend. One room of the trailer's jam-packed now: electronic parts, and motors, and projectors…"

"I get the picture. I did the same thing with chemical equipment, back in my science-fair days."

"And where is it now?"

"In storage with my rock stuff, back in Mount Laurel."

"Mine was all in my folks' garage. They said if I didn't get it out of there by summer, it was going to the dump."

"So you brought it all here?"

"Just what I wanted to keep. Brought the last load three weeks ago.

"Besides, the trailer's just sixty-five a month. For ten bucks, I'm not moving everything again!"

"I guess you've got a point. Well, somebody's bound to rent Thorson's place sooner or later." My shirt collar was pressing painfully on the back of my sunburned neck. I reached up and ran a finger under it.

"Nick, I just thought of something. Alaine said, if

Suzanne or I had any questions on...certain subjects...to ask either one of you. Could I ask you a question now?"

He looked around us, verifying all the nearby tables were empty. "Ask."

"What do you know about hypnotism?"

"Not too much. Why?"

"My roommate tried to hypnotize me last night: because I couldn't sleep and I was turning over and over, distracting him from studying. I don't think it worked, really. But maybe it did help me get to sleep."

"Looked into it a little a few years ago, but I'm no expert. What did he do?"

"He had me stare at a smiley-face sticker on the wall, and breathe deeply, and count the breaths backward from a hundred. And while I did, he kept talking: telling me to rest and relax..."

"Pretty standard technique, from what I've read. The swinging-watch business is mostly for stage acts. But you're wrong if you think it didn't work."

"What do you mean?"

"You relaxed, didn't you? And finally went to sleep?"

"I guess so."

"But you hadn't been able to, before?"

"No. The sunburn was itching too much, and I was too hot."

"See? Hypnotized, you could ignore it. Did you expect him to make you think you were a chicken, and have you lay eggs?"

"No. I really didn't know what to expect."

"Jack, do you watch television?"

"Once in a while. Why?"

"Anything strange happen when you do?"

"No. Should it?"

"What's hypnotism?"

"Relaxing, and letting somebody else drive for a while?"

"Sort of like that. Relaxing, and taking your mind off outside reality for a while. Getting all wrapped up in a TV show, or a good book, is a mild form of hypnotism. Turning off reality, and living what's in the book or on the tube instead. It's no big thing."

"Then some people spend most of their lives, hypnotized?"

"**Everybody** spends most of their lives hypnotized!"

"I don't!"

"You never daydream?"

"Well..."

"See? That's self-hypnosis. I'll bet, when we were talking about Thorson's place, you formed some mental picture of it."

"As a matter of fact, I did. Big and dark and

cluttered…"

"Self-hypnosis. You 'saw' it with your Third Eye: your imagination.

"Hypnotism isn't something mysterious; it's something we do all the time. The trick's learning to use it effectively: use it at will, for whatever we like."

"Maybe we should study it, then: you and I and Suzanne and Alaine. Maybe I should borrow Hadrian's book…"

Nick looked at me strangely. "Hadrian? Like the Roman emperor Hadrian?"

I nodded. "My roommate. Hadrian Marsan. Why?"

"Little red-haired guy? Talks a mile a minute? Walks like something's breathing down his neck?"

"Yeah. You know him?"

"I used to. He started out in Double-E – electrical engineering – the year I did, then went over to physics. Didn't know he was still around."

"He's here at least 'til fall. Maybe we should all get together."

"I don't know. Hadrian…well, takes advantage of people. He'll help you any way he can, but you'll pay for it sooner or later. And he doesn't always tell the truth, or keep his promises."

"He seems okay to me. Kind of strange; he has the room full of black-light posters, and he burns candles a lot. And come to think of it, I saw a book on witchcraft on his shelf. Is he one, too?"

Nick looked around again, making sure our conversation was still private. The canteen was filling up now, but we still had a buffer of empty tables around us.

"He'd like to be, I'm sure. He'd be good, too: he'll do anything if he thinks it's to his advantage. But if he ever thought he was putting in more than he was getting out? It'd be Salem Village all over again, for all of us.

"Don't mention it to him! And if he brings it up tell him you don't know anything about it, and you think people who call themselves witches are crazy. All right?"

"What if he hypnotizes me, and tells me to say what I know?"

"He won't, unless he thinks there's something to learn. But let's talk to Alaine about that. Maybe we can give you some protection."

"Does Alaine do hypnotism, too?"

"Something like it… Saw her last night, by the way. Said she'd copied out most of the things for Suzanne. Should probably get together, the four of us, some evening this week. Maybe tomorrow night?"

"Without Hadrian, I assume?"

Nick's face was grim. "Without Hadrian."

"Fine with me. I have a lab 'til six, but I'm free after

that. If you'll check with Alaine, I'll get the word to Suzanne. Seven?"

He nodded, glancing at his watch. "Uh-oh. Got a class coming up in half an hour. Need to review a couple of chapters first. Better run."

"Yeah, me too. See you tomorrow night…where? Farrington lobby again?"

"Sure. See you then."

He left, and I finished off my second sausage biscuit and my coffee, the latter only lukewarm now. As I walked toward Stanford Hall, I thought over what he'd told me of Hadrian Marsan and decided not to ask to borrow any of his books just yet.

My afternoon class was mostly a rehash of the chapters I'd read Sunday: methods for analyzing metal ores and alloys, preparing us for tomorrow's lab session. The material was dull, and Doctor Preston's droning voice would have been a good aid for self-hypnosis. When the class was over I headed for the Student Lounge and bought a Coke for the caffeine in it, wishing the machines there had hot coffee instead.

I spent the afternoon in the Holy of Holies, carefully shaking up Doctor Knight's brown brew with solvents to concentrate the alkaloids he sought, while the Soxhlet device brewed up a second batch. I finished with about half an ounce of chloroform, hopefully holding all the product from yesterday. At a quarter to six I put it in the refrigerator to crystallize, laid my safety goggles aside, and left.

My first destination was the dormitory, where I checked to make sure Hadrian wasn't around. Furtively, then – expecting to hear his key in the lock at any minute – I took down *Hypnotism: Its Power and Practice* and skimmed the first few pages, standing next to the shelf so I could quickly put it back if he returned.

Almost immediately I found what Nick had called "the swinging-watch business": hypnotic induction with a pendulum. Following it was an account of "the Hartland method," closely matching the technique Hadrian had used on me.

I didn't want to spend much more time in his book just then, but I glanced quickly through the opening chapters: "Misconceptions Surrounding Hypnosis"; "Medical Opinion and Hypnosis"; "Who Can Be Hypnotized?" It seemed my own misconceptions were not unusual.

But Nick had been right; hypnotic states were far more common, less mysterious, and easier to enter than I'd ever guessed. Hadrian, too, had told me the truth about what he was going to do. He hadn't used some sinister power to take over my mind, to force me into some unnatural mental state. He'd simply helped me relax enough to do something I'd done countless times before without even realizing it.

From that point of view, Hadrian wasn't a hypnotist. Nobody was. At most, he was a skilled helper; I'd hypnotized myself. With that as a start, perhaps I could follow his example and learn to help others.

I quickly reviewed what I'd read, making sure I understood it thoroughly, then put the book back on the shelf and left the room, headed for town.

Charlie's driveway was empty. Could he have taken Suzanne somewhere? But I knocked, and after a minute or so there were quiet footsteps inside. The door opened. Suzanne stood there, her face very red above a white bathrobe. "Jack! Come in."

"I was worried about you. Are you all right?" I held out my arms to embrace her.

Suzanne backed away. "Please do not touch me. I am sore all over, and as red as a stop light. If it begins to hurt any more, I may scream. But aside from that I am all right, I think. Are you?"

"Pretty much. My back and rear end are the worst." I looked at her more closely. "Actually, you don't look so bad."

"You see only my face; it was used to the sun already. But other parts of me..." She bent and pulled up her robe to mid-thigh. "See?"

The skin was crimson. "Ouch! That's worse than

any of mine."

"I did not go to my classes today. I stayed here both yesterday and today, and have spent most of the time in the bathtub. With very cold water!"

"Did you sleep all right last night?"

"I slept not at all last night; I could not. But I think that I fell asleep, for a little while, this morning in the tub."

"That's awful. What does Charlie say about all this?"

"He is quite understanding. I told him that you and I had gone to the lake Saturday, and had stayed too long. But he does not know that it was a private 'lake' which we visited, nor has he seen how much of me is actually burned. Our secret is safe!"

"That's good. I looked for you in the canteen today, but I ran into Nick instead. He said Alaine's copied out most of what she promised you…"

"Of what she promised us, Jack. You will study it with me, will you not?"

"Yeah; I'd love to. We're going to try to get together tomorrow night at seven, where we met Saturday: to get the stuff, and maybe talk it over a little. Is that all right with you?"

"It is all right with me…provided that I am better by then. Right now, I feel as if I had just returned from a walking tour of Hell!"

"Suzanne, my roommate tried something last night that helped me sleep. Maybe it would help you, too."

"What is it?"

"How much do you know about hypnotism?"

"Almost nothing. I once saw a show in which some people were hypnotized, and helped to stop smoking. But I have never studied it."

I explained to her what Hadrian had done, and what I'd learned from Nick and from the book. "So, even though I didn't notice anything strange when he did it, I guess it worked. I slept all night, and I feel a lot better today."

"And you think that it might work for me, also?"

"I'd like to try it if you're willing. At least it might help you sleep better than you did last night."

"Then please do. I would be asleep now if I could find a way. And I cannot afford to miss two days of class in a row."

She led me back to the bedroom which now was hers. "Turn your back, Jack. We are not in church, and it might bother you…" There was a rustle, then a creak of bedsprings. "All right. Now you may look."

I turned back to see the bathrobe on the floor and Suzanne in the bed, a pained look on her face as she adjusted the cover. Her arms shone lobster-red against the white sheet. "Should I lie on my back, as you did?"

"That's fine. We should have less light, though.

May I turn off this lamp?"

"Yes. The light from the hall will be enough…and I can look out through the window, at the light over the neighbors' side door. Would that be as good as a smiley sticker?"

"Probably better. Now breathe deeply, and count your breaths: starting at a hundred, and coming down…"

Sitting on the edge of the bed I tried to talk as Hadrian had, droning on and on: "Let my voice be like waves on a shore, or like background music, helping you to relax…as you continue to count…" Meanwhile, I kept counting her breaths myself: afraid she might reach zero in the count before falling asleep.

But I must have been doing something right. Her eyes closed almost immediately, and she'd barely reached the low seventies when her voice fell silent. A moment later she was gently snoring. Just to be sure I kept up the "background music" for a minute or so longer, adding some suggestions that by tomorrow most of the pain and soreness would have gone away.

Suzanne slept on, giving no sign that she heard me…but in the dim light, now, I thought I could see a faint smile on her face. I bent forward and kissed her very lightly on the forehead; then, picking up her discarded bathrobe, I hung it on a bedpost. "Good night, Suzanne," I whispered, and closed the door, and let myself out of the house.

I stopped off at the Lair on the way back for a turkey sandwich and a beer. By the time I'd finished it was almost nine, so I headed back to the dorm.

Yes, Hadrian was there: textbook, notes, black light, candle, Iron Butterfly oozing from the speakers. At least he had the volume turned low. "How's the sunburn?"

"Better tonight. I don't think I'll have any trouble sleeping."

"Good. I'm glad my treatment worked."

"I thought you said you weren't a hypnotist."

"I'm not. But who is? At least I could help when you needed it."

"Sure. And thanks." I undressed, hung up my clothes, and crawled into bed. Tomorrow would be a long, long day.

12 The Critical Censor

May 25, 1971

One more morning I slept late, with no alarm clock to startle me out of my dreams…and, as sometimes happened when I was able to wake at my own pace, I remembered something of the night's wanderings.

I'd been walking down that long road on Alaine's Tarot card, under the Moon. But the pavement had been brick, brilliant yellow even in the moonlight, and

I hadn't been alone. There'd been a pigtailed Dorothy who spoke with a French accent, and a dark-furred Lion, while the Good Witch Glinda had walked beside us, blonde and golden-eyed...

The rest was gone.

I rose and examined my burns in the mirror. The red was fading now, and most of the soreness had retreated to my shoulders and buttocks. I showered, dressed, and sat down – finding I now could do so without wincing! – to read more of *Power and Practice.*

The author, an English hypnotist named Peter Blythe, suggested hypnosis occurs when a specialized part of the conscious mind is bypassed. Though he never precisely defined this "critical censor", nor hypnosis itself, as I read on I recognized it as just another mask, formed from common sense, prejudices and opinions. Wearing it, he said, we sacrifice many abilities: to shut out pain, or call up memories half-forgotten, or control body processes normally thought involuntary. Hypnosis moves the mask aside, letting us regain those lost powers.

This, I decided, was definitely a subject to investigate more deeply, with or without Hadrian's help. So I read on and on...until at a chapter's end I glanced up and saw it was well past eleven. I'd have barely enough time for a sandwich and coffee at the Student Union before class.

The Moon Path

Today's session with Doctor Preston was no improvement over yesterday's. He droned on and on about titrations, redox indicators and the dangers of perchloric acid. I'd already read all that in the text, and some was a replay from a course last year at Rutgers, so I paid but scant attention. Instead, I pondered what I'd been reading in Hadrian's book.

The chapter on "hypnotic aids" had particularly fascinated me. Our back-porch light and happy-face sticker had been primitive next to the flashing lights, metronomes and rotating spirals Blythe had described. By the end of class, my notebook page may not have contained much chemistry...but the margin held the diagram of a motor-driven spiral disk, along with a list of parts I'd need to build it.

From class we went directly to the laboratory, where Doctor Preston issued us chips of stainless steel to analyze. The procedure was simple as such things went, but tedious: first dissolving the chips in acid over a Bunsen burner turned low, then testing samples of the green-brown liquid to see how much it held of iron, of chromium, of vanadium, of cobalt, of nickel. By the time I'd finished all that, it was nearly six-thirty. Hastily I cleaned up my lab area, put away the chemicals, then hurried away to South Campus.

Again all three of them were waiting when I arrived; obviously none were incapacitated by the sun, and

Alaine had gotten the word. "What kept you?"

"Too much chem lab. Doctor Preston's trying to cram in the whole semester's worth of labs in six weeks. Today we did stainless steel. Next week it's brass...but maybe the method's easier."

"Terrible. You would think that they could choose the experiments which you do, so that you could learn it all from just one."

"You'd think so, but they don't. I guess they think by doing everything two or three times, we'll learn it better. Or they're trying to show us what it's like in the real world. You take something real, like brass or stainless, or the limestone we had last week: pull it apart, then sort it out atom by atom!"

"Could just be trying to teach you chemistry's not a great way to earn a living? Otherwise wouldn't they be out somewhere doing it, instead of teaching it here?"

"They do a lot of it right here when they're not teaching. At least Doctor Knight does."

"Sounds like you do all the grunt work for him, the hours you have to work in that lab!"

"It's what I get paid for. It was that, or settle for a B. S. – and have you ever seen the odds on getting a job in chemistry with just a B. S.?"

"No. Pretty bad?"

"About the same as a snowball's, you-know-where."

"Same in physics, from what I've heard. Wonder what Hadrian's planning, come fall?"

"Who's Hadrian?"

"My roommate this summer: Hadrian Marsan. Nick knew him, too, a couple of years ago...

"I don't know what he'll do, Nick. Probably go on to grad school, here or somewhere else. What's the physics department like here?"

"Don't know. Probably about average."

"If he wants a **good** physics degree, he should go to M.I.T. or maybe Georgia Tech. Who ever heard of Calhoun?"

"We all did, obviously. And Doctor Knight did..."

"Thought he just moved here to retire."

"Well, he did, I guess. But he hasn't pulled the plug yet, and it's been six or seven years."

"And you came because he'd pay you to do his chemistry for him."

"Yeah. ...Why did you?"

"Because it's a good agricultural school, and Aunt Theda said I should. The horticulture program's second to none. Suzanne?"

"I came because it was close to Arborville...and because Great-Aunt Clarisse is helping to pay for it. And you, Nick?"

"My dad was an electrician, liked to tinker with stuff, but he never went to college. When he saw I had the knack, he scraped up the money to send me. Had to be in-state for the low tuition. We looked at S. C. State a while, but Calhoun has a better double-E department."

"I thought you were working your way through yourself."

"I am now. No more help from home after I blew it before! Got a job down at Connor's TV-Radio: one to five, weekday afternoons. That's why I'm just taking one course this session. And when I can, of course, I put on the light show."

"Too bad you can't make a living from that alone. It's good."

"Not enough demand around this place. Now, in California…"

"Welcome to the Bible Belt, Nick. Around here, the hippies all have to wear masks!"

"Don't we all?"

"Except in places wild and lone…"

Raising a finger to her lips, Alaine gestured toward another group which had just taken the table next to ours. "Speaking of that, why don't we go up to the room now? I think we might be more comfortable."

So after buying drinks from the vending machines near the foot of the stairs, we rode an elevator up four floors – Farrington Hall's lobby seemed to be a *rez-de-chaussée* – and walked down the corridor to Room

405. Alaine unlocked it, and we followed her in.

Like Hadrian, she'd decorated the room to suit herself…but her decorations were alive! Potted plants were everywhere: on the window-ledge, on the floor, on the bookshelf, and on the back corners of both desks. Leafy vines grew up a trellis rigged against the window; the pane was wide open behind them. A small aquarium full of bright-colored fish sat on the desk Alaine wasn't using for studying.

Obviously she had no roommate this summer.

"You've got quite a jungle here, Alaine!"

"Thanks, Jack. But it's no jungle. You can still see the walls…"

"A good place to take off your mask!"

"And swing through the trees on a vine?"

"Nick, if you swing from a single one of my vines…"

"Sorry, *Rom*-lady. Not enough room in here anyway."

"What are the fish?" Suzanne was staring raptly into their tank.

"Those little green ones that shine are neon tetras. And the orange ones are swordtails."

"They are beautiful."

"Beautiful, but dumb. You've got to keep the lid on tight, or the swordtails will jump right out and die."

"That would be too bad. But what is this strange

little one, sitting on the bottom? The silver one, with black dots?"

"A spotted cory: a kind of tropical catfish. It's the janitor; it cleans up the fish-food the other ones miss, and whatever else sinks to the bottom. If the snails don't get there first."

"Hell of a way to earn a living."

"Not too bad, Nick…if you happen to be a catfish."

"Thanks, but no thanks."

"How long have you had them?"

"Close to two years, some of them. I started with a pair of swordtails, a half-dozen neons, and that same little catfish. Now there are nine swordtails…and can you count the neons? I can't anymore."

"But still, just one catfish. Why not get him a mate?"

"Who says he's a he?"

"Can't you tell?"

"No. Can you?"

"Maybe they could at the pet shop. Somebody must raise these…"

"I asked, but they didn't know."

"Too bad. Poor little fish, all alone." Suzanne sat down on the bed beside the tank, as if to keep it company. I settled next to her.

"Yeah. I know how it feels." Alaine smiled sadly and sat opposite us.

"Missing Carl?"

She nodded. "But at least we had some time together. And, the Gods willing, we will again."

"Heard from him lately?"

"Not for a month now. I'm really worried. The last I heard, they were close to the front."

"He'll come back all right. Just wait and see."

"I know: I have to have faith. But sometimes it's hard."

"Too bad you can't read the cards about him. Sure hope they were right about Dawn."

"They usually are…if we're just smart enough to figure out what they're saying!"

"They were right, when they said that you were the Hermit!"

"Why?"

"Because I so badly needed a guide. And you were the only one who could have helped me. And now…" she raised her canned drink, still unopened… "now I am in the Three of Cups!"

Nick raised his own. "Hear, hear!" Ripping off the pop top he poured Pepsi down his throat, then made a face. "This stuff'll do, but it sure isn't wine!"

"Should I bring some wine? When next we go to the quarry?"

"Not a bad idea."

"Suntan lotion would be good too. I heard you and

Jack both got fried!"

"Yes, it was very bad. I had to stay home from classes yesterday. But I am much better now. Thanks to Jack."

"Glad it worked. I added a little to what Hadrian did for me…"

Alaine looked hard at both of us. "Nick tells me your roommate has been practicing hypnosis without a license. Have you, too?"

"I guess so. Why? Is it dangerous?"

"It can be, if you don't know exactly what you're doing. You can get somebody in big trouble if you say the wrong thing. The subconscious mind takes things very literally. And you can get in legal trouble if you treat medical conditions without a doctor's approval."

"I've been reading a book on it…"

"Books aren't enough. You need to use common sense, too…and a little more. Now what, exactly, did you do?"

I explained how Hadrian had helped me get to sleep on Sunday night, then summarized my own experiment with Suzanne the following night. Though nodding from time to time, Alaine said nothing until I'd finished.

"It sounds pretty harmless so far. But before you do it again, or let Hadrian try it with either of you, I suggest you both finish reading that book. And any others you can get your hands on."

"Nick...I borrowed Hadrian's copy this morning when he was out of the room. Do you think it's safe to let him know I'm interested in hypnosis...without mentioning witchcraft at all?"

"Probably wouldn't hurt anything now. Of course you're interested; you just had first-hand experience. It'd be suspicious for you **not** to show any interest! Alaine, don't you agree?"

"Yes. As long as he doesn't find out about your 'other' interests! But maybe we can find a copy in the library."

"I was thinking about that today, but I didn't have a chance to go look. Maybe tomorrow."

"Please do. I'd like to read it, too."

"Alaine...Nick said you might be able to work out some kind of protection for me. So if Hadrian does hypnotize me, he can't get me to tell him anything about those... 'other' interests."

She smiled. "Jack, what did we do at the quarry?"

"Swam, and got sunburned...and set up a Circle, and took that oath of secrecy..."

"The Oath of the Sanctuary. Jack, I know you and I trust you...and I trust the Oath, too. I'm willing to bet you won't break it, no matter what Hadrian does. But the best protection, for now, is not to let him hypnotize you again. At least not until we've all read the book, and we know Hadrian better too."

"Do you want to meet him?"

"Later, maybe. Not just yet. Let me think about it, and read the cards…"

"Tonight?"

"I don't think so."

"Why?"

"Jack…there are certain times when I try not to use the Art unless I have to. And this is one of them."

"Wrong time of the month?"

"You could say that. Not mine, but the Goddess'. Yesterday was the New Moon."

"So?"

"The Old Religion teaches us to use the power in us, and in nature. The phase of the Moon governs the flow of that power, and how it works.

"The Waxing Moon is a time of growth and creativity. It's easy to do constructive work then, like spells for a good harvest or success in business…"

"Spells? I thought you said that was part of the 'smear campaign'! You can't really turn Christians into toads, can you?"

"No, Jack. The Art doesn't work that way.

"It lets us do a few things we couldn't otherwise, by harnessing our will and faith and imagination. That usually takes some physical act: doing and saying things that symbolize the intent, to help the mind focus on it. That's all spells are. Some are traditional: handed down through the centuries, like recipes. Others, we design ourselves when we need them – but following rules that were old when our ancestors came out of the caves.

"We'll talk more about spells later. All you need to know right now is that they work – sometimes – but you could usually get the same results some other way, with a bit of luck. Nothing that violates the laws of Nature. No instant toads!"

"Good. There's not much Methodist left in me, but what's there was getting worried. And there's too much scientist in me to believe you can just reach out, say, and turn straw into gold!"

She nodded. "That wouldn't work. You could possibly make it seem like gold, to a few people for a short time. That's called 'casting a glamour.' But even that would violate the Law.

"I was telling you, though, about the phases of the Moon.

"The Full Moon is a turning point; the power peaks then. Witches usually meet when the Moon is full. It's easiest then to use the Art, and to contact the Goddess.

"After that, it's downhill. The Waning Moon is a good time for what we call 'spells of diminishment': to get rid of a bad habit, or mice in the barn, or make warts drop off. Those outside the Law cast spells then to harm enemies: diminish their health or their property."

"Then there really are 'wicked' witches?"

"Jack, there are always people who abuse power, and the Art is no different. We're careful who we teach, because there's always the temptation to use the Art at somebody else's expense. But once in a while somebody slips past us…and gets in a lot of trouble."

"What kind of trouble?"

"What we call the 'rebound' effect. If you do good for other people – more accurately if you cultivate love in yourself, so you'll do good without even thinking about it – then you seem to attract good back to you. But if you cultivate greed and hate? Some say 'whatever you do, returns threefold'."

"Remind me not to cast any evil spells."

"Better not cast spells at all at the New Moon, unless there's a real emergency. It takes too much energy, and you could make yourself sick by trying. Aunt Theda made it a rule to 'stay mundane' within two or three days of the New Moon, and I do the same."

"But the cards don't need spells to make them work, do they?"

Again, she nodded. "A spell, yes, but turned inside out: what we call a 'divination.'

"A spell takes power, molds it with symbols, and sends it out into the world to influence things. A

Jack Peredur

divination lets power come in **from** the world, past and present and future, and affect symbols we've set up for the purpose: symbols we then can interpret. Like cards with pictures on them."

I thought of Hadrian and his interacting wavicles. "So when you read the cards, they come up the way they do because the whole world is casting a spell on them?"

"More or less. It's like taking a picture and developing it. You can take pictures all day and develop the film all night, but if light doesn't come into the camera, or the developer doesn't work, all you'll get is black pictures.

"And at the New Moon, every picture you take seems to come out black."

"Like what I was doing in the lab today: analyzing those steel chips for the metals in them. But if I'd started with something else – say, Doctor Knight's 'coffee' – or used the wrong chemicals to pull it apart, nothing would have worked."

She smiled. "Jack, we might make a witch out of you yet."

"Alaine, this is all fascinating, and I know Suzanne's decided to join you. But I still can't just say, 'I'll be a witch, too.' Part of me is too much a scientist, and says spells and Tarot cards and power from the Moon are nonsense. And another part remembers just enough from Sunday school to say if it does work, it's nothing I want to monkey with!"

"I wasn't pushing you. I know a lot of this is hard to accept. But you're already on the Moon Path; I think you know that as well as I do. You met Nick, and me. And at the same time, you met Hadrian. Maybe he's the one who has to satisfy your 'scientist' part."

"I guess it'll just take time. I'm learning a lot of new things, but I can't get it all past my critical censor yet. You've got me half-believing in Tarot cards now, and maybe even spells…though I still can't quite accept why the phases of the Moon should affect them. And Hadrian practically proved he's clairvoyant last week, using good solid math and a different kind of cards.

"If I can just take those ideas and get my mind to build a bridge between them and the science I know…maybe I can get the critical censor to relax a little.

"And maybe then, Alaine, I'll be ready to join you."

13 Sun and Moon

May 25, 1971

Suzanne had been listening in silence to our conversation. Now she laid her hand on mine. "Jack, I know that it is difficult for you. I can never go back and be a Christian: not now, when I have found this other way, this Moon Path. But it is not so for you. You can go back if you like, and be a Methodist again, and forget all about us."

"Hey, Suzanne, I didn't say I'd leave. I just need more time to think about it."

"You said before, that when Alaine has the things ready for us to read…and Nick said that they would be ready tonight, I think…you would study them with me. Is it still true?"

"Of course! Alaine, are they ready?"

"They are. It took a whole evening to copy them out…but here they are." She opened the desk drawer beneath the aquarium and took out a thick little book, its covers painted emerald green, with the card design of the High Priestess on the front in black and silver.

"What's that?"

"The book?" She held it so we could see the cover design. "This is my *Book of Shadows.*"

" *'Shadows'*? Why?"

"It's the traditional name: 'shadows' in the sense of 'spirits,' or 'the unseen world.' I've kept one of these since I was fourteen, and copied all the spells and rituals into it."

Now I recognized the book under the paint; it was a ledger like some I'd seen in the bookstore. "Did you paint the cover?"

She nodded, smiling.

I reached for it. "May I?"

"Sorry. I swore to Aunt Theda I'd never let anybody else read it but another initiated witch. And right now,

I'm the only one I know of!" Taking some folded sheets of paper from inside the front cover, she closed it again immediately. "That's why I copied all this out for you. It's the only way you can see it before taking the big plunge."

"I'm sorry."

"There's no reason to be. Here, take these. They're yours now. Just be sure nobody else sees them!" She handed us the folded papers, putting the *Book of Shadows* back in the drawer.

Suzanne took them, unfolded the top one, and held it so we could both read it. It was titled "CHARGE OF THE GODDESS". Below were several paragraphs in Alaine's tiny, precise writing:

> *Hear the words of the Great Mother, Goddess of Moon and Sea, the Stars and the Mysteries beyond Night and Death: She Whom worshippers of old called Hecate, Aphrodite, Diana, Kerridwen, Rhea, Morganna, and many other Names:*
>
> *"I Who am the Soul of Nature, I Who am the Earth's green beauty, and the Moon's silver wheel among the Stars, and the dark Abyss of Night as well, I call to your own Soul: 'Arise, and look into My face, and know yourself My child and forever a part of Me.' For through Me all*

living things are born, and to Me when weary must all return through Death to be born again.

"Yet to arise and find Me, you must know first the Mystery.

"Seek Me not in church or temple built with hands or tools, for dead walls of stone, however gilded, can never hold Me. Seek Me not in cloisters of denial. Seek Me instead in your heart's own temple; in the night's dark silence; in green cloisters of Nature; in the rhythm of song and the welcoming arms of a lover.

"Come to Me not in harsh robes of penitence, in garments which bind and hide and proclaim your body shameful, for they are but tokens of slavery. Cast them aside! Be free in body, in token your spirit is free as well. For old or young, male or female, your skin is My own rich livery, and the Wise are not offended.

"Call My Names with song and rejoicing, wine and feasting and love, in a place wild and lone beneath the Moon when it is full. Or if that is not safe, speak them silently within your own heart's temple. Either way, I will hear.

"Listen then, if you are alone, for My voice within your heart; watch for My vision before your inmost eye. But if you are gathered with others, and one of them as My Priestess invites

Jack Peredur

Me, then may I descend into her body and for a little while walk among you, answering your questions and teaching the Mysteries: the lore of spell and rune, the Circle of Rebirth, the spirit eternal, and reunion with loved ones beyond Death's door.

"To serve Me strive always for love, and for love alone. All else will follow, for all acts of love and pleasure are My rituals. Sacrifice neither gold nor blood, for both are naught to Me. Share with Me instead your joy, for I am with you and within you always. Worship Me in all you do, through honor and humility, reverence, love and compassion for all things living.

"For Mine is the joy of the spirit, and joy on Earth as well. And My only Law is Love."

"Is this not what you were quoting at the quarry? About loving all living things…and coming naked to the rite, to show that you are free of all laws but the Law of Love?"

"That's where it came from. There's a rhymed version, too; it's on the sheet under that one. I like it for rituals because it 'chants' well, but it says about the same things. And this prose one's better for study."

Suzanne turned the page, read briefly, then nodded. "I will study these both, then, when I have time. And perhaps on Saturday, we can discuss them. I am sure that I will have many questions." Then as she turned another, I saw her eyes widen. "What is this, though? 'The Horned God?"

"Yes. Some witches picture the God as the 'Lord of Beasts.' Human, but with horns and hooves. Like Pan."

"But that is the way Satan looks! With horns, and the hooves of a goat!

"So, Alaine, you told me once but I must ask again. And please – in the name of God, or the Gods – do not lie to me. Do witches worship Satan? Do you?"

"No, Suzanne. Satan-with-horns came from the same place as those witches who turn Christians into toads. Just from some priest's imagination! The Bible describes Satan either as an angel, or as a lion. Centuries later, to scare people away from the Old Religion, the priests said the God of the witches was the same as their Satan, and most people believed it.

"But it was a lie! We don't even believe in Satan."

"You do not believe that there is a God of evil?"

"There are demons, certainly. But no supreme Devil. Not in the Christian sense."

I'm afraid I smiled. "Demons?"

"It isn't funny, Jack. Demons are real, and people have really messed themselves up using Art they didn't understand. Calling up demons, on purpose or by mistake, with no protection. Some died. Others..." She shook her head. "…Just weren't so lucky.

"Demons are like lions: big and smart and usually hungry. They only come out of the jungle if there's easy prey in sight. If you set out bait, though, you'd better be well-prepared.

"Witches don't do that, no matter what Huson says. They're too dangerous. Usually they've got nothing you'd want anyway, unless you're a black magician. They can be powerful weapons, but they'll as likely destroy the sender as the intended victim.

"There's no one, biggest, most powerful King Lion somewhere, though, that rules all the others. And it's the same with demons. Nasty, but not well-organized."

"If there is no Satan, though…and if demons do not come unless you call them…how can there be evil in this world at all?"

"Suzanne, what is evil?"

"Evil is anything which is against God's law."

"And what is God's law?"

"There are the Ten Commandments…"

"Aren't those just special cases of two basic Laws: to love God, and to love your neighbor?"

"I suppose so. Yes: Christ said so Himself."

"And if we don't know those laws, what do we do?"

"We break the Commandments. We steal, and lie, and kill…"

"So 'evil' is in all of us. But it's no more than

ignorance combined with selfishness. It's what happens when we forget the Law of Love: when we put our own welfare above that of others."

"But that is the idea of Original Sin: that we are born in evil, and only God can save us!"

"That's true, I guess, to an extent. We do have to learn, gradually, how to live by the Laws. But it's not as if God were using it as some kind of admission fee. It's just nature."

Suzanne was nodding. "I think that I understand. I have believed in Original Sin all my life…but it has never seemed something which a loving God would inflict on us. Yet, could God have made a mistake?

"What you have said, though, makes sense to me. And many things which I did not understand, now are falling into place."

Alaine smiled at her. "I was brought up Christian, too: a Presbyterian 'til I was twelve. But there were always things that never made sense to me. They said God was all-loving, and all-powerful, and had given us free will. But then they said we'd all go to Hell if we didn't do exactly as we were told!

"Then I went to live with Aunt Theda, and she explained it differently…and I became a witch. But I'll admit it: the first time she mentioned the Horned God, I reacted just like you did!"

Suzanne laughed. "I understand now that He is not

Satan. But why do you think of God in such a grotesque way? From where did His horns come?"

"He's had them a long time. Remember, Christianity has only been around a couple of thousand years. The Old Religion goes 'way back to when people still lived in caves.

"Back then, the role of men was to hunt food and bring it home. So the Father was identified with the hunt, and the prey He could grant to the hunters. He became the Lord of Beasts, the Lord of Nature, with the horns and hooves of the animals He ruled. There are cave paintings showing Him that way, some of the oldest paintings in the world. But the Greeks and Romans used that same image for the Great God Pan, the Lord of Wild Places. And we still use it today."

"Then He is the Father of all of us? But at the same time, the Lord of the forces of Nature which we cannot control? That, I find a little frightening."

"That's not surprising. We see the Horned God as our Father, just as the Goddess is our Mother. But to very young children, what's a father like?"

"I was always a little afraid of my father when I was young. He seemed so big and strong, and he would punish us when we were bad. And much of the time he was away, and we were not allowed to visit him in the cabinet shop. He said that the tools and machines there were far too dangerous."

Alaine nodded. "So Father-Gods are big and strong, and dish out punishment if you break the rules. Look at Jehovah in the Old Testament: 'Thou Shalt' and 'Thou Shalt Not' any time you turn around. And woe to whoever does, or doesn't! It's the same problem kids have when they live with single fathers. Too much discipline; not enough loving care.

"The Old Religion accepts both, of course: Father and Mother. They're supposed to be equals. Yet we feel closer to Her than to Him, like children usually feel closer to their mother than their father. The mother is there to fix their meals and play with them and change their diapers. Often, the father's only home in the evenings. He's just as necessary…but more distant, and more frightening.

"So we cry to our Mother to feed us, and keep us safe, and bandage our hurt fingers. And I hope we remember to thank Her when She does. But we only see our Father at special times: when He leaves for work, or gets home in the evenings, or has a day off. Those are the eight Sabbaths, spaced around the year.

"Or if you prefer, you can think of Them as Sun and Moon: two of Their oldest, most universal symbols. The Moon is always near, driving the tides of the ocean…and of power…and of our bodies. Her light is gentle, and we can look straight at Her, and stay out with Her all night if we want to, with nothing to fear.

The Moon Path

But the Sun is fiercer and further away. If we try to look at Him, He dazzles us…and if we get too close to Him, or stay too long, we get fried like you did last weekend. Without Him, though, nothing could live! And like the Sun, He comes and goes with the seasons.

"So we rejoice with our Mother when the Moon is full, and try not to ask much of Her when it's new. But we meet with the God just eight times a year: to mark the stages of His journey, and ours, through the cycle of time."

"And those are what you call the Sabbaths?"

"Yes. I've given you a diagram on one of those sheets…yes, that one." The sheet held the drawing of a wheel with each of its eight spokes labeled:

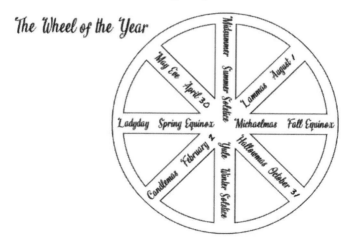

The Wheel of the Year

May Eve
April 30
Midsummer
Summer Solstice
Lammas
August 1
Ladyday Spring Equinox   Michaelmas Fall Equinox
Candlemas February 2
Yule Winter Solstice
Halloweenmas October 31

"They're at the solstices, the equinoxes, and four other days in between. You already know two of them. Yule is Christmas...though ours comes earlier on the solstice, usually December twenty-first.

"And Hallowmas is Halloween!"

"But those are holy days of the Catholic Church, as well. Hallowmas is All Saints' Eve!" She looked over the list. "And Candlemas, also: February second is the Feast of Purification, and candles are blessed as a part of the Mass. Are all of your Sabbaths, then, Christian holy days?"

"They might be. I didn't know Candlemas was a Church holiday 'til just now, but that makes sense. These dates were sacred long before Christianity started. So it would make sense for the Christians to use the same days...and be sure their people were safely in church, not out celebrating naked in the woods!"

Suzanne laughed. "And four of them end in 'mas,' as well: 'mass,' as in church? Five, if you include Christmas as Yule. Did witches then borrow these from the Church, as camouflage?"

"I'd bet money on it. Adapting to fit new times and stay hidden: 'for the Craft must ever survive'."

"You show Midsummer's Night as the solstice. Is that not coming soon? And should we meet for it? What is done then?"

"Midsummer's the time when covens meet together. But we don't even have one coven, yet. And it's the best time for handfasting: the way witches get married. Even the Christians have kept the tradition of June weddings!"

"Yes, but none of us are planning one...and as you said, there are no covens to meet. So, what are you planning to do?"

"Nick has asked to enter First Degree then: to dedicate himself formally, before the Gods, to be a witch. He's been studying for months getting ready."

"Studying things copied from your *Book of Shadows?*"

"That, and some other books I've lent him: Sybil Leek, and Paul Huson, and Lady Sheba..."

"Paul Huson?" She'd mentioned him earlier, and I thought I recalled the name from Hadrian's bookshelf too. "Didn't he write *Mastering Witchcraft?*"

"Yes. Have you read it?"

"No, but Hadrian has a copy. I've been meaning to look through it."

"Huson got the theology pretty garbled, but he has some good pointers for developing 'magic' powers. That's what most of the book is about."

"Casting spells?"

She nodded. "They're not our main reason for existing, the way he seems to think. But we do use them from time to time, and early on we need to learn how they work. What to do with them…and what to avoid doing!"

"You mean hurting other people?"

"That, and working at the wrong times, or without protection. Actually, Huson's sort of a hypocrite about harming others. He gives all sorts of warnings, but then fills up a whole chapter with some pretty effective curses. He even tells how to call up demons!

"But he gives another full chapter of ways to protect yourself if things go wrong. And his formula for casting a Circle is one of the best I've seen…even if I'm more comfortable with Aunt Theda's."

"I guess he wanted the book to be complete…"

"Well, there's a lot left out, and I've found several mistakes. You can tell he learned most of his lore in a library, not a Circle. But it's good basic material just the same. I wouldn't recommend trying his spells: not until you've given the basic principles time to sink in, at least. And certainly not his demon summonings, ever! But it certainly wouldn't hurt you to read his book."

"Could we look at your copy? Borrowing Hadrian's would be pretty obvious."

"Nick, have you finished it yet?"

"Sure have. Still things in there I'd like to copy out, but that can be later. I'll bring that, and Lady Sheba, with me Saturday."

"Who's Lady Sheba?"

"A Priestess who published her *Book of Shadows,* or part of it. It's a complete round of Sabbath rituals, along with a set of Laws that date back to about the Seventeenth Century. Ways to keep outsiders from finding out you're a witch, mostly, and to keep harmony in a coven."

"**Published** it? But I thought only another witch could read a *Book of Shadows!"*

"She says the Goddess told her to make an exception: to publish hers for whoever wanted to read it. So she did. There was quite a scandal when it came out. And it's terribly repetitious. She uses the same chants over and over, and writes them out in full each time. But some are very good...and not much different from the ones Aunt Theda taught me."

"Interesting. We'll have to study that one, too. But I don't understand. The Goddess **told** her to publish it? How?"

"I think that I understand, Jack." Suzanne reached for the first sheet of paper she'd laid aside: the one with the prose form of the Charge on it. "Here. It says, '...But if you are gathered with others, and one of them as My Priestess invites Me, then may I descend into her body and for a little while walk among you.' Alaine, does that mean that the Goddess takes over the

Priestess' body, and speaks with her voice?"

Our Priestess nodded. "I think so. I've never tried it, and though Aunt Theda saw it happen she never experienced it herself. But she said there'd be a definite change in the woman who did it: as if Somebody Else were looking out through her eyes and using her voice. And that Somebody would tell them things the woman herself couldn't possibly have known."

"So that 'Somebody Else' came to Lady Sheba, and told her to publish?"

"I guess so. Actually, all I know is what she says in the introduction. But whatever happened, she's given us a great reference book."

"That's another one I want to read, then. And what was the third book? The one Nick still has?"

"Sybil Leek's *Complete Art of Witchcraft*. It's half as thick as Huson, but there's twice as much meat in it. I think it's the best of the three. It's not rituals, not stuff dug out of a library: just life, as it's lived by someone brought up in the Craft. And again, in a tradition not too different from Aunt Theda's.

"Huson gives you the basics of the witch's powers, of spells and divinations. Lady Sheba gives you the Sabbath rites. But those are both special cases. Ninety-five percent of the time, you won't be doing either one. Sybil gives you that other ninety-five: what it's like to be a witch on a daily basis. I won't try to sum it up now, but it's a book you need to read."

"Nick, how much longer will you need that one?"

"Hardly started on it, really. But I read fast. Maybe another week; two at the most."

"That would give us, still, two weeks in which to study it ourselves before the Sabbath.

"I am still not certain that I am ready. But, if I decide that I am, Alaine – if I can learn to accept the idea of a God with horns, along with the Goddess – might I pledge myself along with Nick?"

"That's rushing it a little. Aunt Theda said the English witches watched and tested her for more than a year before they even let her become a Novice – much less brought her into First Degree!"

"Yes, I can understand why. Because she might still, secretly, have been working for the Church?"

"Or just a bad risk. Somebody who'd use the Art unworthily."

"But do you think that I am either of those?"

"Working for the Church, no. As for the other? I don't think so. But I need to know you pretty well before I'll be comfortable with it.

"I'll make you a deal, though. If you can convince me you're ready by then, and if the cards agree, you can come into First Degree at Lammas. And that goes for both of you. All right?"

"All right. And with you, Jack?"

"Sure. That leaves the rest of May, and all of June and July. By then, I'm sure I'll be ready to give you a yes or a no."

"Good. And in the meantime, Alaine, we will study all of these sheets. And read those books, and whatever others you have, which might help us.

"But now, it is almost nine. And I have an eight-o'clock class tomorrow, and a chapter yet to read before it. And Jack came to us directly from his laboratory. Did you even have time to eat?"

"I grabbed some crackers from the machine in the Student Lounge. Ate them as I walked over."

"That is not a meal. We should leave, and let him get some real food. And we will see you down in the lobby, on Saturday morning at nine, will we not?"

"Same time, same place. ...Nick, they brought the wine last week. Since you so clearly don't like Pepsi, would you get it this time?"

"Sure, Rom-lady. I'll see you, Jack, Suzanne..."

So we left Alaine's jungle, and as Nick's motorcycle thunder died in the distance I started back with Suzanne toward Charlie Blake's.

"...And you're really going through with it? In spite of the Horned God?"

"Yes: if Alaine says that I am ready, and the cards agree. ...Oh, Jack, it is not as if I will walk through some door which will close forever behind me. Even if

I join and you do not, we can still be friends…"

"Well, I've never said I wouldn't join. I just need to know more: to read Alaine's books, and the things she copied out for us. By the time I've gotten through those, I should be ready to decide."

"Then why do you not come in with me tonight? I will fix something for us both to eat, and we will read the sheets together."

I was tempted – oh, God and Goddess, I was tempted! – but somehow the chemist in me won out. "Suzanne, I'd love to. But I have studying to do, too. Doctor Knight's due back tomorrow, and he hinted there might be a pop quiz on those chapters he assigned."

"Yes; you told me, but I had forgotten. So why do we not meet tomorrow instead? Come as soon as you can leave Doctor Knight's laboratory. And we will read these things together then."

"I'll plan on it, Suzanne."

We were at the door now. She turned the handle, opened it a crack…then turned back to me. "Blesséd be, Jack."

I bent and kissed her forehead gently. "Blesséd be." Then she was gone, and I started back toward food, and books, and bed.

14 Purgatory

May 26, 1971

Doctor Knight had returned from his conference on schedule, and started class Wednesday by passing out copies of the paper he'd presented: "Studies on Rearrangement Following Nucleophilic Addition to Quinazoline-3-Oxide." The lecture that day was the presentation he'd made in Philadelphia, with slides.

I was relieved, since the pop quiz I'd been dreading

hadn't materialized. At the end of class, though, he called me to the front of the room. "Mr. Peredur, I'd like to go over your master plan for the synthesis. Is it ready?"

My stomach sank. I hadn't worked on it at all while he'd been away. I reminded myself, though, that he'd seen it only once before, a crude copy drawn from memory, and I'd put in a week's work since then. "There are still some areas that aren't clear, but I think I've mapped out most of it."

"Very good. Can you be in my office at two?"

I'd have to go there directly from Doctor Preston's class. The timing would be close, but I could make it if I hurried. "I'll plan on it."

Nodding, he dismissed me.

I spent an hour in the Holy of Holies going back over the plan, added some marginal notes, then went to the Student Union for lunch. None of my friends were there, though, so after a quick meal alone I hurried back to Stanford Hall to do a little more work before class.

Doctor Preston stood and droned for two hours about the methods and uses of reductive titration. Then it was time for my meeting with Doctor Knight.

To my disappointment, when I laid the chart in front of him he frowned. "Is this your current version?"

"Yes. I put the latest changes on it just hours ago."

"I wish you'd copy it over. This isn't very neat."

"I know. This is only a working copy."

"Very well. Now show me how you propose to make the compound. Walk me through the steps."

"There are two possible approaches. I could make the pyridazine ring first, and work from that end. Or I could start at the other end: make a substituted indole, then build up the pyridazine on it atom by atom…"

"…Well, I think you've done well in mapping out your syntheses", he told me at last. "As a guess, I'd say your second approach has a better chance of working. I've had experience with most of the steps you propose, and can recommend them.

"But in the first approach…" his finger jabbed at one of the synthetic steps I'd diagrammed. "Here. You've built the partial ring system with a carbonyl group, so it will condense with aniline. But more likely it will rearrange like this…" and beside the structure I'd drawn, he sketched another. "So when you run the Bischler reaction, the ring won't close."

Looking closely, with a sinking feeling I realized he was right. "I'm sorry. I should have seen that myself."

He nodded. "It's always the small things we overlook. So, while you finish extracting those passion-vine leaves, I want you also to redraw this chart neatly in ink. Show the second approach only, for now. Make two copies: one for your research notebook, and another for my own files.

"Have you started your research notebook yet?"

"No. What should I use? How's it done here at Calhoun?"

"Go to the bookstore and get one of their bound ledgers: the large size. From now on, record everything you do in it, and date it. Each step of your process on a separate page. And everything in ink!

"As for the new chart: draw it on drafting vellum, the large sheets they have in the bookstore. Use black ink, and a template for the ring structures. It must be neat! Then fold it and glue it permanently into the notebook. The bookstore has everything you'll need.

"Then, when we've discussed it again, perhaps you can start on the actual synthesis…"

I nearly asked him what possible difference it could make, whether I redrew the chart now or waited until the synthesis had been proven. But I bit my tongue. After all, I was being paid to do it his way!

So swallowing my irritation I went back to the Holy of Holies and fired up the Soxhlet extractor again with a fresh batch of passion vine. When it was finally running smoothly, I walked over to the campus bookstore and went looking for the supplies Doctor Knight had recommended.

I'd been in the store only once before, on the first day of classes. It had been very crowded that day, bustling with activity as everyone else bought textbooks too. Now, though, it was almost empty, so I decided to look around a little before I left. The extractor would surely run well enough unattended until I got back.

Having seen them before, I found the blank ledgers easily. But the vellum wasn't with the typing and graph paper where I'd expected to find it. Might it be back there in the corner, near that rack of many-colored posterboard?

The aisle led me past a rack of used paperback books, topped by a sign proclaiming "50 cents – 3 for $1." I almost walked on by, but one on the top row caught my attention. "*TELEPATHY*," its title screamed in white against a black and orange background…and the author's name was Sybil Leek.

A book on Hadrian's favorite subject, and written by Alaine's witchy mentor? That was too strong a coincidence to ignore. So I stopped, took it from the shelf, opened it, and scanned the table of contents. It seemed to be a "how-to" manual…and the final chapter, I saw, dealt with hypnotism.

Curiouser and curiouser! Could Someone have put it there especially for me to find? I still doubted that, but after the past few days I could no longer dismiss the possibility. And maybe this book was just what I needed to build that mental bridge between science and magic. So taking it with me, I went on into the back corner of the store.

The vellum was there, in a choice of sizes and grid designs, and the opposite wall held a large rack of assorted drawing tools. I sorted through templates designed for computer programmers, for architects, for engineers: templates of the Greek and Roman alphabets; of electronic symbols; of ellipses, circles, and squares; of tree and bush silhouettes; of pneumatic and hydraulic parts…and, finally, of the hexagons and pentagons I'd need to draw my molecular diagrams. I took one of those from the rack, chose an eleven-by-seventeen-inch pad of vellum printed with a square grid, on second thought reached out for another, then went to pay for it all.

As I'd hoped, the extractor was still running smoothly when I returned to the Holy of Holies. The brew underneath was already a rich brown, but the dripping liquid still had a faint yellow tinge so I let it continue.

By six I'd made a good start on the first of my charts, pencil-sketching the structures of my starting materials and several intermediate compounds. There'd be plenty of time, I hoped, during the rest of the week to finish the layout, then go over the sketches with ink and fill in the lettering. But now, Suzanne awaited me.

I saw with satisfaction that the fluid dripping from the thimble was now colorless. This batch of "coffee" was done, and would be ready for re-extraction and concentration tomorrow. Turning off the heat and straightening up my desk, I left the Holy of Holies with my new book in my hip pocket.

Charlie's door opened as I approached. It was Suzanne. "Hello, Jack!"

"Hi. Have you eaten?"

"No. And I hope that you have not, either. Are you hungry?"

"Yeah. Want to drop by the Lair?"

"I had a better idea last night, but today I have had time to do it all properly. So come into the kitchen…"

There was a pie on the counter, browned on top and still steaming from the oven. Two small pie shells full of something yellow, topped with dabs of whipped cream, waited nearby. A pot of soup simmered gently on the stove, and beside it bubbled a small saucepan of something thick and brown and redolent of mushrooms and garlic. On the table stood two glasses already filled with red wine. Beside each was an empty salad bowl, and between sat a larger bowl holding lettuce and celery, apples and raisins and nuts, chopped and mixed and covered by some white dressing.

"Wow, you must have been working all afternoon! It looks wonderful. You shouldn't have gone to so much trouble, though!"

"Jack, it was no trouble. I love to cook, when there is time. In Mortagne I would often cook for the entire family. My mother was too tired, after spending all day with the younger children! After that, this was nothing." She spooned salad into our bowls.

"…There are no foods here which you cannot eat, are there? I am sorry; I did not think to ask before I cooked. Do you have allergies? Myself, I get a red….?" She gestured to her face, her cheeks. "Little bumps, everywhere!"

"A rash?"

"Yes. …When I eat lobster, or *crevettes*. I am sorry, I do not know the word." She pantomimed instead, pretending to bite into a raised, hooked finger.

Something curved, then, and finger-sized. "Shrimp?"

"I think so. Or crab. Asparagus, also. And you?"

"Indian food, curry and stuff like that, makes my nose run and my head close up. Like a bad cold, except it's gone the next day. Probably it's one of the spices they use.

"Except for that, and a few odd things like pistachios, I can eat pretty much anything."

"Well, then, you are in luck. There are no strange spices here: only onions and garlic."

I laughed. "Asparagus and lobster, and exotic

spices! Not the sort of things starving students need to worry about much."

"*Starving? Mais, non!* Clarisse has promised to send money every two weeks, and today her first check came. I was not expecting it until Friday, at the earliest. So, I am rich! …At least, *un peu* rich." She held up a hand, her thumb and forefinger about a dime's thickness apart.

"I'm glad you have money. I won't get paid for almost a week yet – not 'til the first of the month – and I'm running low. Can you believe I had to pay fifty dollars for that Chem 801 book?"

"No! How could a textbook be so costly?"

"Limited edition. I guess all graduate-level books are expensive, since they don't get to print very many. And that's a thick one. We'll never get through it all in this summer session. I guess Doctor Preston wants to try, though."

"Is he the one who lectures so boringly?"

"Yeah. He ought to take up hypnotism himself… Suzanne, this salad is delicious!"

"Thank you… But no, he should not. If anyone is to hypnotize me, it will not be Doctor Preston, and it will not be Hadrian Marsan either. It will be you!"

"But I thought you were over your sunburn."

"Not entirely, but I am much better. And also curious, after what you did Monday and what I heard last night. So, could you try something else with me tonight: after we eat, and study Alaine's papers?"

"You want me to try hypnotizing you again?"

"Yes. I know that it can be used to cure bad habits, like smoking…or eating too much! So I would like you to help me with my own bad habit."

"Food? But if you enjoy it…"

"I enjoy it a little too much! Jack, have you noticed that I am fat?"

"Remember what I said about Rubens?"

"I remember. And in the Library I looked for a book of his paintings, and found it. They are beautiful. But I am fatter than any of those women!"

"I don't think so…"

"You do not look into the mirror every morning with me. And you do not carry around with you, all of this extra weight.

"Jack, I thought that perhaps it would not bother me much, to have you see me at the quarry without my clothes. But it did. In Paris I was not so fat; it all came after…after Richard. Perhaps I thought that by eating more, I could better stand the loss…the loss of my dreams. And help to keep away the guilt."

"I've heard that called 'anxiety eating'. Can hypnosis cure that?"

"It may be my last hope. I have tried diets, but I do not have the will power to stay on them for long.

The Moon Path

Perhaps if you could simply have me eat less, at each meal?"

"I guess we could try. But this is a strange way to start a diet!" The blended smells of the courses to come were already making me drool.

"Jack, this meal is my farewell party for food: as, in the Church, we observed 'Fat Tuesday' – *Mardi Gras* – before the forty days of Lent. With your help, I would make this my own 'Fat Wednesday.' So that perhaps forty days from now, I will be less fat!"

"Mardi Gras? I thought that was a New Orleans festival."

"They took it from the Church, and made of it something for the tourists. I have heard that the city becomes one great party! …But this, tonight, is mine. Whatever may come, I am going to lose weight. But I think that with you helping, it could be much easier."

"All right. I still haven't finished the book, but I've got the basic principles, I think…"

She brought the soup to the table in separate bowls, each covered with light-colored cheese melted and baked in place. I dipped into it…and the cheese wrapped itself around the spoon in one big sticky glob.

"No, Jack. Try it this way." She cut into the surface with the edge of the spoon, near one edge. The spoon came away with a morsel of warm cheese in it, and none on the bottom.

"I think it's too late." I shook the spoon, but no cheese fell off. So I held it like a lollipop and nibbled the cheese off. "Tastes great, though, regardless!"

"I should have warned you. But wait until you try the soup. It is my grandmother's recipe."

Her grandmother, I had to admit, had been an expert. And then came the meat pie – another family recipe, she told me – and the mushrooms served up on the side, and after that the small dessert pies, *tartelettes* filled with a cool lemon custard.

Stuffed with food and mellowed by the wine, we piled the dishes in the sink. "I will wash them later. But now, we have our reading to do." Carrying the bottle, now less than half full, she led me back into the little bedroom and sat down on the bed. "Come here, Jack. Sit beside me."

I hesitated. It had been with exactly those same words – "Come here, Jack. Sit beside me!" – that Judith had started our first torrid night together: textbooks swept aside, the student suddenly the tutor. Was Suzanne about to do the same? And was I ready, so early in our friendship?

"Oh, Jack, are you stalling once again? Do you think that I am trying to do to you, with the wine, what Richard did to me with brandy?"

I banished the thought. "No, of course not." *Liar!* "But what if Charlie comes home? What will he think?"

"We will both have all of our clothes on. Let him think whatever he wants to!" She reached under the pillow and pulled out something folded. "But if we were out on the couch I would have no warning, and nowhere to hide these papers. Here, I can put them back under the pillow. And if he asks, we were simply talking about… About what?"

"Classes, I guess. Whatever Nick and Alaine were talking about, Saturday night while we ate."

She smiled. "Repair of motorcycles, I think. But you do not have a motorcycle."

"Should I get one?"

"No. You would look strange on Nick's, I think. And I would look still stranger, riding with you."

The thought of her pressed close behind me, arms around my waist for mile after mile, certainly had its appeal! "Not so strange. And it would be transportation, at least. It's a long walk from here to the mountains."

"Do you mean the mountains of the Sleeping Giant? Or those on the card of the Moon?"

"Either one. I had the strangest dream the night before last…" and I told her about the Yellow Brick Road and those who had traveled it with me.

To my surprise she didn't know *The Wizard of Oz*, so I briefly summarized the movie for her. "…And then Glinda sent her back home. Using the magic that had really been there all along."

"And you dreamed of me as Dorothy? And Nick as the Lion?"

"Yes. And Alaine, of course, was Glinda."

"Then who were you?"

"Myself, I guess. Why?"

"You could not have been either the Scarecrow or the Woodman. For it is clear that you have a brain, but you have a heart; also. Or you would not have stayed that first day to help me in Stanford Hall."

"I guess I just can't stand to see a damsel in distress."

"That may be. For in distress I certainly was!" She unfolded the papers Alaine had given her. "So: if we are to reach the Emerald City, should we not study the maps?"

The top sheet held the Invocation of the Horned God, whose title yesterday had upset her so. Tonight, though, she seemed to take it in stride.

Under that title, Alaine had written a few paragraphs of explanation:

> "Like many Eastern religions, and Christianity before the Fifth Century, the Old Religion teaches the doctrine of reincarnation.
>
> "There exists, somewhere, an eternal

Heaven: the Home of the Gods. But few who die enter it. Most go instead to the Land of Youth, where souls rest before entering new lives. In time they will be born again, in this world or some other.

"There is no eternal Hell: only the Borderland – the "Threshold of the Gate" – where the wicked must wander in darkness until their evil is spent and they may enter the Land of Youth.

"The Horned God – some call Him Kernunnos or Karnaynas, "the Horned One" – is the Keeper of the Gate of Death, and the Judge of Souls. It is He Who decides how soon a soul may enter. In this aspect, He may be asked to mediate between the world of the living and the spirits in the Land of Youth or on its Threshold.

"At Hallowmas – Hallowe'en – the Gate opens wide, and for a time the spirits of the departed may return to share invisibly in a feast held in their honor. From this belief come <u>ALL</u> the modern traditions of Hallowe'en."

She had written that last "<u>ALL</u>" in capitals, heavily underlined. There followed a blank line, then the Invocation itself:

"Dread Lord of the Gates of Death! On this night of remembrance and feasting, open wide, we pray You, those Gates through which all souls must pass, that our dear ones may return this night to make merry with us.

"And when our time comes, Giver of Peace and Rest, may we pass those Gates gladly: fearing neither Your judgment nor the darkness before the Threshold. May we remember the sweet Land of Youth which lies beyond. And may we know that, rested and renewed in spirit, we will be born again by Your grace, and by that of the Goddess.

"Let that rebirth be in the same time and place as our dear ones, that we may meet again, and know, and love each other anew."

Suzanne was nodding. "I was always taught that this life is our only one on Earth: that we come from the hand of God, and go at death to either Hell or Heaven. Or possibly to Purgatory, if our sins may be forgiven through penance after death.

"But it has always seemed so unfair: that some might live only a few years, or perhaps never at all…like my baby. Yet that would be their only chance to be on Earth, while others might have seventy years or more.

"Perhaps, if what we just read is true…the soul of my baby may be born again to someone else. Jack, do you think that it might be so?"

"I don't see why not. We studied other religions the last year I went to Sunday school, and one thing most had in common was the belief in reincarnation. Christianity had it too, until the elders at Nicaea took it away. People love to pick and choose what in the Bible they'll take literally and what they won't. Maybe when Christ said we have to be 'born again' to get into Heaven, that was a literal part."

"I have never understood how a loving God could send us forever to Hell: could make a world which could turn us so much toward evil, that not even He then could save us. But if Alaine is right, He did not. That was only one more creation of the priests!"

"That sounds kind of like the old question: 'Can God create a rock so heavy He can't lift it?'"

"Of course He can. God is all-powerful!"

"Then why is He struggling, trying to lift that rock?"

"Oh. It is a trick question. And whatever I answer, it is wrong?"

"Now you've got it. Can God make a world so evil that even He can't save the souls it ruins?"

"Yes, and no. But if God is both all-powerful and all-loving, He did not even try. So, can there be no

Hell? But if not, are we all to enter Heaven? No, for that is reserved for the saints, those who have lived all of their lives by the Law of Love. So all others must go to Purgatory…"

"Or more likely, get born again on Earth. 'Purgatory' might be right here and now. So they can have another shot at Heaven…and another…and another…"

Her eyes were very wide. "It **fits!** …But why, then, did the Church stop teaching this?"

"So they could scare you with Hell, I guess."

"But this is terrible! Almost all which I was taught about God, seems now to have been lies by the priests. I know that God cannot be evil. But a God Who would send souls to Hell, when He had the power to save them, would be no different from Satan!"

"Maybe Alaine's right, then. And maybe all our ideas of Heaven and Hell, and Purgatory too, are just memories from the Land of Youth and the Borderland. The nice in-between place, and the not-so-nice one."

"I wish that we had some way of knowing before it is too late. Should we believe all which the priests have said? Or only part of it? Or none? I wish that we were able to remember…"

"Have you ever heard of Bridey Murphy?"

"No. Who is she?"

"Nobody anymore. It was a famous case back in the

Fifties, I think: a woman who was hypnotized and remembered another life. I don't think there was any proof Bridey Murphy had really lived. But a lot of people who hadn't believed in reincarnation before that, started to wonder."

"Do you suppose that we, too, could do that? Could you help me...?"

"Sue... May I call you that? 'Suzanne' seems so formal, now!"

"Please do. It can mean that we are good friends. One more mask taken off!"

"Thanks, then; I will.... Sue." I savored the feel and sound of it in my mouth.

"So, Sue. Let's try one thing at a time. You've already asked me to help with your diet. And the only thing I've ever done before with hypnosis is put you to sleep. I can't promise any of those other things."

"Still, I want to try. If I truly can remember a life before, it will mean that Alaine is right and the priests were wrong. So perhaps, when I am thinner...?"

"Maybe. I need to read that book of Hadrian's... Oh, guess what I found in the bookstore today?"

"Another copy?"

"No. But it's on Hadrian's favorite subject...and by one of Alaine's favorite people!" I produced it from my hip pocket. "What do you think of that?"

"Telepathy: The Respectable Phenomenon. May

I?"

"Sure!" I handed it to her.

"This is by the woman…the witch…who wrote the book which Alaine so recommended: the one which Nick is still reading. And telepathy is…speaking, with your thoughts?"

"Pretty much. Sending them from mind to mind."

She studied the table of contents. "And this last chapter is about hypnosis!" And she started turning pages, looking for it.

"Those three subjects just naturally seem to come together: hypnosis, past lives, and ESP. Blythe's *Power and Practice* has a chapter toward the end on 'Hypnosis and Reincarnation.' I skimmed it one morning when Hadrian was away. It tells about Bridey Murphy, and some other cases too. But at the end, Blythe mentions some other ways 'hypnosis and the occult' are related…and he gives some examples of telepathy, and clairvoyance, and precognition. It seems like all the forms of ESP are easier under hypnosis."

"Does Hadrian know this?"

"I'm sure he does. It's his book."

"But he does not have a copy of this other one?"

"No, I don't think so. Why?"

By now she'd found that last chapter and was skimming it. "According to this, hypnosis is not so harmless as Hadrian told you. A person could use it to control another if he wanted to, and if he were very good at it.

"Nick seems to think that Hadrian is that sort of person: that he would use it that way if he knew that it could be. Now I know that I do not want him to hypnotize me. And I do not think that he should hypnotize you again, either."

"Sue, what he did with me was just what he said he'd do. Nick may be right about him, but I haven't seen that side at all. You're right, though. 'Til we both know him better, I guess we should keep alert.

"But if he could do that, couldn't I? Are you sure you still want me to hypnotize you?"

"Yes. I trust you." She handed the book back to me, folded the papers, opened a drawer in the dresser, and thrust them under a layer of underwear. "And I will read no more tonight. I am ready right now. Are you?"

"I guess so."

"Then let us do it. I want to stop being fat! And if you think that remembering other lives, or learning to read each other's thoughts, is too much to do in the same night? Well, there will be many other nights. And perhaps we will do all of that.

"But now…should I undress, and get into bed, as I did last time?"

I thought again of Charlie, and what he might think if he walked in on us. "Only if you're ready to call it a night. It's not even eight o'clock yet."

"Then you will wake me up after it is done?"

"Sure, I'll bring you out of it. But you don't really go to sleep, you know, unless somebody deliberately tells you to. Blythe says that over and over again. The only thing that goes to sleep is the critical censor!"

"Very well. I still have the dishes to wash, anyway, and the kitchen to tidy."

"I can help you with that…"

"But you will not! Do you not have homework still to do?"

"I need to read another chapter for Chem 801. But I can do that tomorrow, between classes."

"No, Jack. I will wash the dishes, and you will study! But first, let us finish what we have begun."

Suzanne lay down on the bed and doubled the pillow under her head to prop it up. It was still bright outside the window, and the porch light next door, our focus point last time, was turned off. The TV antenna above it caught the setting sun's last light, though, and glowed as if on fire. She pointed at it. "Should I look at that, this time?"

"Sure, if it doesn't hurt your eyes. Ready?"

"I am ready when you are."

"Then breathe deeply, and count your breaths…. Let my voice be like waves on a shore…"

15 The Gold Mist

May 26, 1971

It took longer than before: maybe because Suzanne wasn't exhausted this time, or because tonight there was less sunburn pain to flee. By the time our countdown had reached forty, though, her eyes had closed.

By then, too, I'd thought of a possible approach to her problem. If I could have her "live" the experience of eating and seeing herself grow fat, then fasting and watching herself thin – all in compressed "hypnotic time" – it might impress the deeper levels of her mind more than words or conscious wishes ever could.

For that, though I'd have to send her deeper than I had before. So I decided to try something else I'd found in the book: the way of the visionary journey.

"Now I want you to imagine yourself standing at the top of a stairway. Soon you'll start to walk down. And with every step, you'll feel yourself growing more and more relaxed…"

Going down the stairway, I hoped, would help deepen her trance. After that, I'd have her continue the journey to a table with food to devour or refuse, and a mirror in which to see the results. If there were a door at the bottom of the stairs, and a room beyond…

"Down, another step, and another… And now, as you descend, imagine that you see a door ahead of you, at the bottom of the stairs…"

Suddenly, then, she gasped in surprise: gasped, then spoke, her eyes still closed, quietly but with deep feeling. "Oh, *mon Bon Dieu.*"

"What happened?"

"At first, everything was…hazy. Not real. A step; a step. Leading straight down, I thought, like stairs in a house. I was building the picture in my mind, little by little…

Jack Peredur

"Then suddenly it changed: became real, not hazy at all. I am there now, truly **there,** as much as in any place ever. Seeing it all. Feeling the stairs under my feet." She was speaking faster now, as if fully awake again save that her eyes remained closed. "And it is quite different from what I had imagined. The stairs are carpeted in rich deep yellow, thick and soft underfoot. And now they curve. And the walls are stone."

The method, I thought, must be working. "Great! Can you see the door yet at the bottom?"

"Yes. It is partly open. And beyond is golden light…"

She was going too fast for me. I'd meant it to be a closed door, one behind which I could have had her find the table and the mirror. Well, maybe I still could turn these images to my purpose. "Beyond it there's a room, and in the room, there's a table…"

"No! You cannot see it as I can. I am trying to see it as you say, but it is too real now. I no longer can make it change."

Blythe hadn't discussed this possibility! Where were these images coming from? At least they seemed harmless enough, so far. "All right. Then tell me what you see."

"I am at the bottom of the stairs now, and looking out…and it is outdoors. There is thick mist but it glows as if sunlit, turning everything golden…"

Ravenwood: A Seeker's Memoir - Book 1

"Does the mist mean something special to you?"

"Yes! It is like the morning mist in Normandy, all glowing as the sun first began to break through. I loved to walk in it, for it made the world seem a place of magic, and all of my troubles far away. It made me feel safe."

"What else do you see?"

"The ground before the door is smooth and grassy: grass growing up from a smooth under-carpet like moss with small flowers in it. There is no path, but I do not need one. Now I am walking through the door, and out into the mist." She smiled, eyes still closed. "The moss is wonderfully soft under my feet, and cool."

"Go forward, then…" Maybe I could make the table and the mirror appear outdoors here, on the grass. "Look ahead of you, and in a minute you'll start to see some shapes appearing through the mist. There will be…"

But her dreamy voice interrupted me again, jumping ahead. "Yes; I see them. And suddenly I know this place. They are the old stones!"

"Stones? What stones?"

"Stones which were set up many centuries ago: no one knows by whom, nor why. In Normandy, there are many such. People call them *menhirs*. Some say that they were for worshipping the Devil, but to me it never

Jack Peredur

seemed an evil place. I suspect, now, that it was for
worshipping the God and the Goddess."

"Was this a real place, in France?"

"Yes: deep in the *Forêt de la Trappe,* beyond
Tourouvre. 'A place wild and lone,' as Alaine would
say. Most people feared them, but I would come here
often. I did not believe in their magic, not really, but I
always felt calm and safe here.

"In France they had trees around them, but here they
stand alone. Apart from that…. Yes, they are just the
same."

"Can you describe them?"

"They are very old, rounded by weather. One stands
half again as tall as I, but it leans a little. The other lies
flat on the ground. Perhaps it once stood also, but has
fallen.

"Near them are nine or ten others, not so large:
standing along a curve, as if there had once been a
complete ring – a Circle! – with these larger ones
inside. And beyond those is one more: standing also,
but not so tall as the one beside me. Perhaps it was one
of the corner markers."

"Interesting place! Like what we helped Alaine set
up in the quarry, but bigger?"

"Yes: twelve or fifteen steps across. I would come
here, sometimes, with a lunch packed – for it was two
or three hours' walk from home – and I would set it on

the flat stone as if on a table, and sit there on the ground beside it, and eat. Perhaps that was its purpose, long ago: the altar, in a church of the Old Religion!"

Food. Food on a table! Maybe I could make this work after all.

"Imagine, then, that you brought food today, and set it out on the stone: enough for a dozen people. Tell me when you can see it there."

She smiled, eyes closed. "It is there! I thought of it, pictured it as vividly as I could, and said, to myself and to whatever Gods might remain here, that I wanted it. For a moment nothing happened. But then the mist grew thick and bright and hid the stone for a moment, and there was a sound, almost like singing. Now it has gone, and there is bread, and cheese, and wine, and a roasted chicken. Exactly what I imagined!"

"Should I eat?"

"Not yet. First, imagine there's a mirror facing you: a large, full-length mirror. You can see yourself in it. Tell me when it's there."

There was a very long pause. "I see it. The mist grew bright again, and brought it. But I cannot see myself in it."

"Why not?"

"I do not know. It is a mirror which was in my mother's room in Mortagne: very old, and set in a wooden frame which stands on the floor. She called it her *miroir de cheval* – 'horse's mirror' – for no reason which I ever knew. But when I look into it I see no horses, nor myself either. Only darkness."

"Maybe that's because you don't want to see yourself in it. Is that right?"

"It may be right: perhaps because I am so fat and ugly."

"Sue, you're not ugly! And if you want to stop being fat, the best way is to learn to see yourself in that mirror. So turn away from it for now, and I'll tell you what you'll see when you look back. You'll see yourself, not as you think you are now, but as you'd like to be…"

"Yes. As I was in Paris, before I met Richard?"

"If that's what you want. And it won't just be in the mirror. When you look down at yourself, you'll be the same as your reflection. …All right, now: turn around and look."

"Oh!" She smiled, delighted. "There was a sudden sort of *shift*, and then things were different. Now I am wearing the very first dress which I made for myself in Paris, and the shoes which I bought to wear with it. And I feel so light, I could almost float in the air!"

"Good! Can you describe the dress?"

"It is of blue velours, with bright yellow piping. It is long but the top is cut very low, and the dress clings to me like a glove…so that you can see how good is my figure!"

"I wish I could see it. But now, I'd like you to pick up a piece of food – anything you like – and take a bite."

"I have torn off a piece from one of the loaves, and I am biting into it. It is very good!"

"Eat all you want, and take as long as you like. But, Sue, time is a little different where you are. So when you hear me say 'now,' you'll have eaten all you want. Do you understand?"

"Yes."

She fell silent, and I watched the sweep hand of my watch as it counted off thirty seconds. "Now. Have you finished?"

"Yes. I ate half of the loaf of bread and some of the cheese and chicken, and I drank some wine. And now…Jack, can we be sure that no one else will come here?"

"If you want that, then let's make it so. Nobody else will ever come there. …Unless we invite them."

"Then may I take my dress off now? As I did at the quarry?"

My mind jumped back to the sight of her there, naked but for her medal, skin dappled by sunlight and the shadows of leaves: pictured her the same way now, but wrapped in golden mist…. *Careful, Jack*! With an effort I wrestled my thoughts instead to ice and snow.

Jack Peredur

The Moon Path

"Sure. But why?"

"I made the dress too narrow on purpose, to make me seem even thinner than I am: like that bathing suit, made more to be seen than to be comfortably worn. Now that I have eaten my fill, it feels very tight indeed.

"And this place among the stones is much like the quarry: 'wild and lone,' but it has always felt safe to me." She laughed quietly. "It would not be the first time I have taken off my clothes here – some of them, at least! – for comfort, when it is warm."

"All right. Get comfortable. Just don't get burned this time."

"I cannot. The mist will protect me."

"I thought you said the sun was breaking through now."

"Jack, this is not the Normandy mist as I remember it, but as often I wished that it could be. It always felt cold and wet until the sun came, and then it would quickly thin and burn away; the 'magic' lasted only a few minutes. But this is warm and dry instead, and so thick! Moving in it is almost like moving in water, although I still can breathe easily. And I feel that it will always be here, filled with this wonderful golden light."

"Wow. I wish I could see it…. Can you still see yourself in the mirror?"

"I can. And though I feel full, I do not look any

fatter than I was when I made the dress." She smiled. "In fact, I think that I look really good!"

Easy, Jack! I tried not to picture too vividly what she must be seeing.

"So now, I'm going to ask you to walk around the two stones…and when you come back, it'll be as if a whole day has gone by. You'll have digested the food you ate before, and be hungry again. And the stone will have fresh food on it, as much as before. Do you understand?"

"I think so. One time around, means that for my body a day has gone past."

"Right. Now go around the stones…and come back to the table, and look in the mirror. You've gained a little weight. Not much, but you can see the difference, can't you?"

"Yes. My stomach is not so flat as it was."

"All right. Now, we're going to speed up time even more. Eat from the table, as much as you like…then walk around the stones again. Each time, it's another day. The food is fresh again, and you've gained more weight. As I count from one to ten, you'll do it ten times…and when you have, you'll be as fat as you are now, in…in the Calhoun world. Do you understand?"

"Yes. But must I? Become fat again, even here?"

"I'm afraid so. But then we'll burn it off again, and plant some suggestions to keep it off. In both worlds."

The Moon Path

I crossed mental fingers. *God – or Goddess? – please, let it work*!

"All right, then. I am eating…"

I looked at my watch again, counting off fifteen seconds for each "day". "One. Two. Three…"

"Ten. Now you're going around the stones for the tenth time. And now, go stand in front of the mirror. What do you see?"

Her voice was thick. "I am…so, so fat now. And ugly." A tear formed, in the corner of her eye. "Everything bulges, and droops.

"Please, Jack, make me thin again!"

"I want you to be. And you will be! Here, and in Calhoun, too. But to do it, you'll need to eat less at each meal.

"Look at the table, now, and separate the food into two piles. Put in one pile just the amount you've been eating each day…and in the other pile, everything else. Tell me when you've done it."

A short pause; then, "I have."

"Now, point your finger sternly at the extra food, and will it to go away."

"I did. And that singing came again, and it dissolved back into mist and vanished!"

"Good. Now, look at the pile you kept…and divide it in half. And then make one half go away."

"It is done."

Jack Peredur   255

"Could you live on half of what you've been eating?"

"Certainly! It still is almost as much as I ate each day in Mortagne."

"Good. Now let's go through ten more days. But now when you come around the stones, there'll be just that much food and no more. By the end of the ten days you'll be used to eating that little again, and find it satisfies you just as well. And with each day, you'll lose a little weight…until at the end, you'll be thin enough to wear your dress again. Do you understand?"

"Yes."

"Then I'll count off the days. One. Two… Ten. Now, look in the mirror and tell me what you see."

"Jack, it worked! I am as thin as before!"

"Do you want to put your dress back on?"

"Must I? For I am sure now, this was a holy place of the Old Religion."

"No. I think you'll be fine without it." Memories came back, Suzanne "without it" at the quarry, but I pushed them firmly aside: *easy, Jack*! "We've probably done all we can for now, anyway.

"So leave the stones, and come back: back to the doorway, and the stairs, and Calhoun…"

"And dishes to wash, and classes tomorrow again at eight, and a body which still is fat. Again: must I?"

"I'm afraid so. Bring your dress, if you like…"

"And the shoes. And the mirror! It should not stay outside. What if it were to rain?"

"I thought you said there'd always be warm mist here."

"Yes. But there are flowers and grass underfoot, so it must sometimes rain also. …There. I have the dress over one shoulder, and the shoes back on my feet for now, since the mirror is too heavy for just one hand. But, Jack, where is the building with the stairs?"

"You can't see it?"

"No, the mist hides it. And there were no buildings near the stones in France. Only forest."

"Follow the sound of my voice, then, and let it lead you back to the door. One, two, three, and you begin to see a faint outline ahead through the mist. Four, five, six, and it's getting clearer. Seven, eight, nine, ten, and clearer still. Tell me what you see."

"It is like another place which I knew in the hills, though far away: an old Norman tower, round and built of stone. That one was all in ruins, but this is not! And in its wall is the door, still open, with the stairs within."

"Very good! Now I'd like you to stand at the bottom. In a minute, I'll ask you to climb back…"

"No! May I not explore a little, before I go back to the dirty dishes?"

"All right. But not very long, all right? And tell me everything you see."

"I have put the mirror and the other things down, at the bottom of the stairs. Now I am looking around.

"The tower has only one room at the bottom, a round room. Hanging in the center, above my head, is a big chandelier of shining brass with many candles burning. The stairs are at my left, curving up along the wall to a landing straight across in front of me. Above the chandelier, everything is dark."

"What else is in the room besides the stairs and the chandelier?"

"There are other candles on the walls, in holders of bronze with glass chimneys. Higher up are tapestries with scenes woven into them, hung in a row circling the room like those movie posters in the Cougar's Lair. On the floor are large chairs of dark wood, two pairs with small tables between; they look very old.

"And there is another door facing me, under the landing of the stairs."

"Is it open or closed?"

"It is closed. May I open it?"

"I'd rather you didn't, this trip. We'll leave it for another time. I think you should probably come home now."

"Very well. But I will leave the mirror here. And I have hung the dress over it, so that it will not be too badly wrinkled if I want to wear it again someday! …And taken off the shoes, and put them under it."

The Moon Path

"Fine. Now I want you to come back to the stairs, and stand at the bottom. Soon, I'll ask you to come up. But there are a few things I want to tell you first.

"Whenever you eat, from now on, I want you to look at the food and decide how much you'd normally eat. Then cut that amount in half. Put the rest aside, and don't touch it. And from now on, until I tell you otherwise, you'll be satisfied with just that half. Do you understand?"

"Yes. I will eat less, but enjoy it more."

"Good. That was what we came here for.

"But while we're here, let's make it easier to get back next time. From now on, when you want me to hypnotize you just close your eyes, relax as much as you can, and then say to yourself…" What would be a good password? "Say 'Gold Mist.' Three times. And when you do you'll find yourself on the stairs again, looking down at the door. Do you understand?"

"Yes. So that we will not have to spend a lot of time, counting breaths."

"Yeah. Then I'll count down from ten to zero, and you'll walk down the stairs just like you did tonight. When I say 'zero', you'll be standing right where you are now and you'll be in this same calm, relaxed state: ready to go on, to explore the tower or go out into the mist.

"But in a minute, I'm going to count back upward

from one to ten. As I do I want you to climb the stairs, back to where you started. And as I say 'ten', I want you to open your eyes. When you do, you'll have come all the way back to normal, waking consciousness. You'll feel great: well-rested, still relaxed, but alert. And you'll remember every detail of what we've done tonight.

"Are you ready?"

"Yes."

"Then, here we go. One… Two…

"…Ten. Open your eyes."

She did, and even in the semi-darkness I could see how they sparkled. "Jack, that was beautiful!"

"How do you feel?"

"Wonderful. But it was all so real!"

"Sure; why not?"

"I would not have expected it to be so: only faint, like a daydream. As it was, at the beginning! But then something invisible seemed to tug and pull me in, and suddenly it all seemed as real as this room around us. I could feel the grass under my feet, and taste the food, and hear the mist singing as things came and went, even as I listened to you here.

"How could anything I was only imagining seem so real?"

"Well, Hadrian would say it's all in your mind anyway. There's nothing out here, really, but whirling wavicles!"

"I do not know what a wavicle is, whirling or not. Nor, I think, do I want to. But I am still amazed by it all." Experimentally, then, she touched her stomach and sighed. "Even if I am not thin here, yet, I believe now that soon I will be. And then, Jack…perhaps you will see me in such a dress as I wore today in the mist."

"I'll be looking forward to it."

"Now, though, I have dishes to wash." She reached up and switched on the lamp. "And you have chemistry to read, before your class."

"Yeah. I guess I'd better go."

"But you will come back, tomorrow night?"

"I don't know. I have a lab tomorrow afternoon, so I won't get to do any homework early. But I'll call you, and let you know if I'm coming. And let's plan on Friday, for sure."

"I will, then. But I will not plan to cook for you another supper such as this one was. From tonight onward, I am on a diet. And I will stay on it, until once again I can wear a dress like that one!" Escorting me to the door, she kissed me lightly on the cheek as we parted. "Good night, Jack. And thank you."

"Glad to help. Good night, Sue."

16 Mindpower

May 27, 1971

Clouds had gathered during the night. They drizzled on me as I walked to Stanford Hall, and by the time Doctor Knight's lecture was over the rain was coming down hard. I spent the time between classes in the Student Lounge, doing homework and munching crackers, and went straight to my afternoon class and lab.

The rain continued. I called Charlie's house from the pay phone at six and again at a quarter to seven, but there was no answer. I still had at least an hour's worth of homework to do, not counting the charts to redraw, so I decided to devote the rest of the evening to chemistry.

It was almost ten when I returned to the dormitory, soaking wet. As I'd expected, Hadrian was there: black light on, stereo playing, candle burning. But tonight he didn't have his slide rule out; instead of working physics problems, he was reading a paperback book.

"Hey there, Jack. Did you just buy this?"

He flipped up the front cover so I could see it: orange and black, with the title in white letters. I couldn't quite read it in the dimness, but I didn't have to. It was *Telepathy*.

I'd pushed it in between two thick chemistry texts on my shelf, hoping he wouldn't notice it. From now on, I resolved, I'd follow Sue's example and hide anything I didn't want him to see at the bottom of my underwear drawer! "Yeah. I ran across it in the bookstore yesterday, looking for drafting paper. Haven't had time to read it yet."

"I didn't think you were interested. Did my demo the other night get you hooked?"

"It did stir up my curiosity. Someday I'll have to go through those books and see just how good the evidence is. I'm still not sure how that 'proof' of your clairvoyance worked."

"Okay. You've never had statistics, have you?"

"No."

"Imagine, then, I have ten pennies." He held one hand closed, then raised and opened it abruptly. "I just threw them all into the air. And now they're coming down." He bent as if watching them tumble and come to rest. "Look! All ten came up heads!"

"I can't see them, Hadrian. But for all ten to be heads, you must have put glue on their 'tails'!"

"Jack, I took all my scores so far and did a little more math. The chances of my doing as well as I have up to now, purely at random, are one in fifteen hundred. That's **less** likely than tossing ten coins and getting 'all heads'!"

"Okay. That kind of 'proof,' I can understand. But someday I need a quick course in how you got that number: how you know it's one in fifteen hundred, not just one in fifteen."

"Sure. Any stats book has tables in the back for that. There's even a set in the *Handbook of Chemistry and Physics*, though they don't explain how to use them. You'd have to know already. Read *New World of the Mind.* Rhine explains it pretty well in there."

"Someday I will: when I have more time."

"Time? You can spend all day at the lake getting

sunburned, but you don't have time to read a book?"

"Sure I do. And plenty else to read now, to fill it up."

He thumped *Telepathy,* now closed on the desk in front of him. "That's why you bought this one?"

"I'll read that, too. But it'll be a while before I get to it."

"Then you don't mind if I read it first?"

I was trapped. "No, I guess not. I need to read your hypnotism book first, anyway, to understand what you did the other night."

"Nothing you couldn't have done for yourself, if you'd known how."

"Maybe. But I didn't, and I appreciate the help."

"Thanks." He took Blythe's *Hypnotism* from the shelf and held it out to me. "Here. Put it with your books. So maybe you'll be more likely to find time."

Accepting it, I pushed it in where *Telepathy* had been.

"You might start by reading the next-to-last chapter. He tells about some interesting studies using hypnosis as an aid to ESP. And the same idea shows up in here." He thumped *Telepathy* again. "Maybe we could do a few of our own."

"It's an idea. But you weren't planning to use me as the guinea pig, were you?"

"We both know you can be hypnotized, now. So

why not?"

I could have told him exactly why not, but it would have given too much away. "There are probably dozens of people on campus who'd be interested, and who have more time for this sort of thing than I do. Why not put up a notice in the Post Office?"

His look of irritation melted into a grin. "Why didn't I think of that? We could form a study group. Run statistical tests, with and without hypnosis, and compare the results…"

"That might be interesting. You could look for ways to unlock the hidden powers…"

The grin widened. "And with a bigger group, we could do more runs in less time…"

"Yeah." And maybe I'd be able to keep my own time free, for Suzanne and Nick and Alaine. "You could meet right here, some weeknight."

"Here. Help me design the notice." He was already digging in his desk drawers, bringing out felt-tip pens and some large index cards. "First, we need a name for what we're forming. 'ESP Research Group'?" He shook his head. "Too formal-sounding; nobody'd come. But 'ESP Club' sounds stupid. How about 'ESP Study Group'?"

"I don't like 'ESP-anything'. Some people may not even know what it stands for. How about 'Mind Powers Unlimited'?"

"A little ambitious. Might scare people off."

"Then something simpler. Maybe 'Mind Power Lab'?"

"'Lab' sounds too much like another course. So: 'Mind Power Group'? 'Mind Power Study…' Aha!" He printed something on one of the index cards, a line of block letters arching across the top, and displayed it:

MINDPOWER!

"Well, it's striking…and easy to remember…"

"And under it, the Zener symbols…" He scribbled some more, then held up the card again with an added square, cross, circle, star, and wavy lines. "Like this. So people who've studied the subject will know what we're doing."

"If they haven't, though, that won't tell them anything."

"Would you rather say, 'Tests will be run according to the Rhine methods, and analyzed statistically'? That might scare people off. If they don't know what these are, they can assume it's just decoration.

"And then, under the symbols: how about, 'How would YOU like…' No, not a question. A declaration!

The Moon Path

'SCIENCE has proven YOU can have...
TELEPATHY! CLAIRVOYANCE! PRECOG-
NITION! Let MINDPOWER unlock these HIDDEN
POWERS within YOU!'" I could hear the capitals in
his voice as he scribbled furiously on the card.

"Has science really proven that, though? Or do just
a few people have them: like the one-eyed man in the
Valley of the Blind?"

"Rhine seems to think everybody does; they're just
buried deep in most. But I don't think he ever tried
hypnosis to dig them out. He mentions it briefly in his
book as 'something that was once associated with the
idea'...then jumps to some other subject. As far as I
know, nobody has ever combined the ideas: hypnosis
to unblock ESP, and statistics to test the results. With
both together, we should get some impressive numbers
fast!"

"You could be right. But you'll need to screen your
people somehow, or you'll have every nut-case on
campus showing up at your first meeting!"

"For the first meeting, that might not be bad. We
can pass out sheets telling just what we're planning to
do, and how. And have just a few card tests, with
volunteers. Then we'll meet again a week later, with
just the ones who decide it's worth the trouble. The rest
– the ones who expected us to hand them powers for
free – probably won't show up."

"I guess it'll work. But will everybody fit in this room?"

"If they don't, we'll move to the study lounge downstairs. If we can evict the card players for a while! Or maybe that storage room behind, if it's open and not too full."

"Okay. How soon should we have it?"

"This is Thursday. How about Friday night, a week from tomorrow?"

"A lot of people might be going home for the weekend. Why not the Monday after that?"

"Yep, I guess that'd be better. That's what: June seventh?"

I checked the little Student Union calendar tacked up over my desk. "Yeah. If you put the notice up tomorrow morning, they'll have a week and a half to think about it."

"I will. And then we can start writing up the handout sheet."

"You'll have to do that, Hadrian. But if you like, I'll read over it and tell you if there's anything I don't understand. Just to keep you from going too far into the math, too soon."

"Thanks. So, we're agreed on the plan?"

"I guess so."

"And on the notice. This, with something like 'Organizational meeting: Monday, June 7; Room F-

The Moon Path

315, Holbrook Hall'? Seven o'clock?"

"Yeah."

"Fine. So I need to write this notice more neatly, now, on another card. Or somebody does; I'm not good at graphics. Are you?"

"Fairly good. But I thought you'd drawn those pictures you showed me: the Freemish cube and the poyt?"

"I wish I had, but no. A friend in physics did them, but he graduated this spring. So can you do the notice?"

"Hadrian, I've been doing graphics half the evening for my research. My hands are tired. Could it wait 'til some other time: maybe this weekend?"

"I'd really hoped to have it up tomorrow morning. Come on, Jack. In the name of science?"

"Well, it really isn't very much, is it?"

"Just the one card. Please?"

"All right. I'll need the pens. And do you have a ruler handy?"

"Here. Red, black, blue…and a ruler. Oh, and yellow too."

"Thanks." Sitting down at my desk, I redrew the design on a blank card. "Like this?"

"Fine. Do 'MINDPOWER' in red. And can you sort of shade those letters, so they seem to stick out of the page? The symbols, too?"

Jack Peredur   271

"I'll do my best, Hadrian…"

It took not one card, finally, but three: the others discarded since he'd thought of "better ideas" even as I'd written. I wasn't happy with all the shading, but it would do.

"Here it is. And your pens back:"

"That's pretty good, Jack! So maybe you can make us a new set of Zener cards, too?"

"I thought you could buy those."

"Not where I got mine. They went out of business two or three years ago. And I don't want to risk my only deck at the first meeting. Like you said, we may have every kook on campus show up!"

"Couldn't you use regular playing cards? I think they're a dollar a pack at the bookstore. Have people guess which suit each card belongs to."

"Maybe. But the statistics aren't as clean as with the Zener cards. There are five Zener designs – not four, and not six – just because it makes the math simpler, and 'sigma' a whole number instead of some fraction. …It's worth a try, though, if I can simplify the math. I'll have to work up new tables, of course…"

"I'll let you do that, then. It's been a rough day, Hadrian. I'm going to bed."

"All right. I'll put up the notice tomorrow, then. And we'll plan on meeting right here, a week from Monday." He turned from me back to his desk, brought out the slide rule from the drawer and began to twiddle it furiously, muttering as he did. "Using four suits gives a 'p' of one-fourth…and a 'q' of three-fourths. So for a whole-number 'sigma', we need…"

But he wasn't talking to me anymore; this new conversation was strictly between himself and the paper he was filling with calculations. Tuning him out, I crawled into bed.

17 Protection

May 28, 1971

Friday at six, I called Charlie Blake's house again. Suzanne picked up the phone almost at once. "Hello?"

"Do we still have a date for tonight?"

"Jack! Yes, of course."

"I tried to call yesterday. A couple of times! What happened?"

"I am sorry. It was raining too hard for me to walk

home. And Charlie had to stay late, printing copies of some tests which he was to give this morning. We did not arrive home until almost eight."

"You were in Stanford Hall?"

"Yes. And I went by the Student Lounge, and the Research Library, and your laboratory also, Doctor Knight's, to look for you. But all were locked, except for the lounge."

"I might have been in the library anyway. They keep it locked now except during class hours; that's why all the chem majors have keys. Did you knock?"

"Yes, but quietly. I did not want to disturb anyone if they were in there studying."

"Sorry. I was around on the far side. Guess I just didn't hear you."

"Well, it does not matter. We will be here tonight! Charlie, also. But I have told him that you will be coaching me with my math problems, so he will not disturb us."

"I didn't know you needed any help: not with math."

"I do. We have to solve simultaneous equations, and I am not good at it yet. Perhaps you can show me what I am doing wrong."

"Are you using Cramer's Rule?"

"No. What is that?"

"A math shortcut I learned at Rutgers. I'll show you

when I get there."

"Thank you. And then we can study the rest of Alaine's papers. And perhaps, if there is time, you can hypnotize me again."

"That's kind of a tall order for one evening, isn't it? Especially if we go out to eat, too?"

"Possibly. But it will not take me long to eat: not since my 'twenty days' in the mist! I had only a hamburger for lunch today, and I did not even want to finish it."

"Good; it must be working. But why don't I stop off and pick up deli sandwiches from the Lair?"

"Certainly. But I do not remember what they have. Is there roast beef?"

"I'm sure there is. On a bun? With brown mustard, and a pickle?"

"Please. And if I cannot finish it, you will be welcome to the rest."

"I may take you up on that. I had crackers for lunch again today.... What about Charlie? Ask him if he wants something, too."

"Please hold the telephone, then, and I will be right back." I heard her retreating footsteps, then muffled voices in the distance. A moment later she was back. "Yes, please. I told him that we were having roast beef, and he also wants one. And a beer: a Schlitz Light."

"Fine. And for you?"

"I will have water, only…and perhaps some wine after the meal. There is still a little left from Wednesday night."

"Fine. And I'll see you in about half an hour…"

The Cougar's Lair was crowded, especially downstairs around the bar and deli. I ordered three roast-beef sandwiches with all the trimmings, then while the man was making them I picked out an assortment of packaged snacks for Saturday's outing. In fifteen minutes I had my order and was on my way to Charlie's.

Suzanne met me at the door. "Hello, Jack! May I carry those in for you?"

"I've got them; they're not heavy. Where should I put them?"

"On the kitchen table. Let me go and get Charlie, and we will eat."

Taking out the sandwiches and the two cans of beer I'd brought, I arranged them on the table for three people. But Suzanne came back alone.

"He says that he would rather wait and eat later, when he has come to a better stopping place in the grading. But he told us not to wait for him. So why do we not take the food back to my room, and eat it there as we study?"

The sandwiches were good, but soon gone. "And now: show me the rule of which you spoke.

Cramer's?"

"Yeah. What's your first problem?"

She copied two equations from a sheet, then handed me the pen and the scratch pad. "These."

$$3X + 4Y = 5$$
$$2X - Y = -3$$

Simple! "First you rewrite them as determinants...."

"I am sorry. I do not know what those are."

"They're just grids..." and I showed her. "Fill in the coefficients; then multiply each diagonal, and subtract. That reduces each grid to a single number. Last you divide, and the answers fall right out. See, here's the solution for 'X'..."

$$X = \frac{\begin{vmatrix} 5 & 4 \\ -3 & -1 \end{vmatrix}}{\begin{vmatrix} 3 & 4 \\ 2 & -1 \end{vmatrix}} = \frac{-5 - (-12)}{-3 - 8} = \frac{7}{-11} = -0.636$$

She shook her head as I wrote. "Jack, that is even more complicated than the way which I have been learning."

"Show me that way, then."

"I must write one equation above the other, just as I did. Then find numbers by which to multiply them both, all of the numbers in them, to subtract and get rid of the X's." She tapped the half-page of class notes from solving a previous set.

I nodded. "Cramer's just takes out the guesswork. Saves some paper, too. …And, here's the solution for 'Y'."

$$Y = \frac{\begin{vmatrix} 3 & 5 \\ 2 & -3 \end{vmatrix}}{\begin{vmatrix} 3 & 4 \\ 2 & -1 \end{vmatrix}} = \frac{-9 - 10}{-3 - 8} = \frac{-19}{-11} = 1.727$$

"See how it works now?"

"I think so. It seems very complicated. But do you simply do the same thing every time? Instead of having to guess?"

"Yeah. Once you've done a few, it practically works itself. And equations in three variables, like these further down, solve the same way. Those are a real bear the way you're doing them!"

"Then let me work the next one for myself." She wrote, scratched her head, wrote a little more, then stopped and looked up. "Is it right so far? And then, I just divide the forty-eight by three?"

I did my best Henry Higgins. "By Jove, I think you've got it!"

Sue proved a quick study, doing the rest on her own. Flawlessly! "And so, it is done. All on just two sheets of paper. And in only…forty-five minutes."

"Great work!"

"But now I wonder: why do they not teach us this method? Instead of the other one, which makes us guess, and guess, and multiply everything, and likely make mistakes?"

"Probably it just wasn't in the textbook. Professors are sort of bound by the books they choose, or that some committee picks for them. Not many have the time or talent to write their own!"

"I know. And perhaps that is good. Think how terrible it would be, to have to learn from a textbook written by your Doctor Preston!"

I groaned. "Dry as ashes, and twice as boring."

"And so: that is behind me. Behind us, I mean. And thank you." She closed the math book. "I can do the rest of my homework later: perhaps on Sunday. For tomorrow, I plan to be doing other things!"

"I got picnic food at the Lair while I was waiting for the sandwiches. Do you like Danish?"

"It is a sweet roll, like a flat *tartelette*? With fruit or jam in the center?"

"Jam or cream cheese, usually."

"I have never had one, but I love *tartelettes*! To make, or to eat."

"I got us half a dozen: cream cheese, lemon, and raspberry. And some crackers and chips." I pulled them out to show. "And a six-pack of Coke. I know Nick said he'd bring wine this time, but it's good to have a choice."

"Yes. I do not think that I, myself, will want any. Not unless the wine which he brings is bad! But perhaps the others will."

I started to gather and re-bag the chips, but she stopped me. "Before you put those back, I have two other things, which are heavy and should go in the bottom. So they will not be crushed."

"I thought you said you hadn't gotten any food!"

"These are not food. Charlie brought them home on Monday. He said that although it was much too late for that first time, we would surely need them again before the summer ended!" She reached into the dresser drawer and brought out a squeeze bottle of suntan lotion. "This is the large, economy size!"

"Good idea." I added it to the bag. "What else?"

It was a spray can of insect repellant. "For the mosquitoes. I had many bites, and they itched terribly that next day. Almost worse than the sunburn."

The Moon Path

That too went into the bag, and she helped me load the chips back on top. "Jack, if you want to leave this bag here tonight I will bring it tomorrow."

"If that's convenient for you?"

"Yes. It will save you from carrying it all the way back across College Hill.

"And so: we will have food and wine, and lotion and mosquito spray to wear, and the God and Goddess will be with us. What more could anyone want?"

"Not much, I guess. But speaking of the Gods, hadn't we better go over the rest of those sheets Alaine gave you?"

"Yes." She reached under the pillow and pulled them out. "I read them all last night. The first two have the way to set up and take down the Circle, and the blessing for the food. She recommends that we learn those by heart. The others are just samples: short prayers to the Goddess for health and happiness, and to the God for strength and success. We need not learn those word for word, but only their general forms. We can plug in the details later."

Taking the sheets from her, I quickly scanned them. Yes, the Circle method was the same one Alaine had used at the quarry. The prayers were short and very much to the point, but there was one thing about them that disturbed me a little. "She asks, and asks, and asks the Gods for favors. But she never says she'll do

Jack Peredur   283

anything in return. Shouldn't there be a balance?"

"I wondered about that also. But then I asked myself, 'what could she have offered?' In the Catholic Church we burn candles, or give money to the priests to say a special Mass. For a great favor, if we are rich, we may offer some special thing: a chalice or a candlestick, to be used in the worship. Or a greater amount of money.

"But all of those are material things: sacrifices given to God, or to the church, which the priests tell us is God's house on Earth. The Goddess says 'sacrifice neither gold nor blood, for both are naught to Me. Share with Me instead your joy, for I am with you and within you always.'

"So what we must give is not candles, nor money, nor things of gold or silver. Instead, we must do a greater thing. We must live by the Law of Love: exactly as Christ told us we must. And that is not a thing which we can do, or not do, as we choose. It is something which we must do always. Or we have not done it at all."

"I guess you're right. I hadn't seen it that way. So, being a witch isn't just something you do when the Moon is full. It's the way you live, and your attitude toward everything, every minute of your life."

"Yes. It is not to kill or hurt or be cruel to other living things, including other people, without a very good reason. And it is not to hate them, nor curse them, nor hold grudges, no matter what they have done. And to help them in whatever ways we can, and prevent others from harming them, if possible.

"Only then can we be worthy, to ask for favors from the Gods."

"That's not easy. I'd like to think I live by that Law already, but I have to admit I do hold a grudge sometimes. There was a physics teacher, my sophomore year at Rutgers...."

"What did he do to you?"

"We had three members of the football team in the class. They goofed off all semester, but somehow skated through with C's. I worked my tail off, and Professor Vernon gave me a D. He marked two problems wrong on the final, that I'd done absolutely right. The answers just weren't in the units he wanted. I showed him, but he wouldn't change the grade: just sneered, and reminded me who was the boss. I guess he needed to keep those footballers up off the bottom of the curve.

"So that semester I got four A's, a B, and that D. The only D I've ever gotten, except in phys.-ed. in high school. I sometimes still wish I could meet him in a dark alley somewhere with a baseball bat...."

"Yes. I, too, sometimes dream of meeting Richard again...and making certain that he would do to no other woman ever again what he did to me. But I think that if we met in real life, and I with the knife in my hand, I would simply walk away."

"I know. And I'd probably never swing the bat, either. But isn't it almost as bad just to enjoy thinking about it?"

"Possibly. It 'hurts none,' but neither does it help us to learn better the Law of Love. If we have within us, always, 'honor and humility, reverence, love and compassion'…how could we also find room for a grudge? Especially, against someone whom we will probably never see again?"

"I guess we couldn't. But even with my 'Vernon D,' my grades were still good enough to impress Doctor Knight. So I guess it's time to let it go, and forget it."

"Are you going to ask the Goddess to help?"

"Yeah. What better first prayer could I say to Her than that? One asking for help doing what She wants anyway?"

"None. And perhaps it is time that I, too, let go my grudge against Richard. Perhaps then I will have more room in myself for the Law of Love. And perhaps She will then be able to show me how to free the spirit of my baby.

"Every night I have said the *Ave Marias* which Alaine assigned to me. But tonight, and every other night from now on, I will add another prayer." She

Jack Peredur

pointed to one of those Alaine had written. "This one. Will you say it with me?"

"Sure. Should we cast a Circle?"

"No, I do not think that is necessary: not for a simple prayer. I have simply knelt, as I was taught as a child, and said mine." She rose then, and turned, and got down again facing the bed. I moved to kneel at her side. She took my hand, holding up the paper so we both could see it, and we spoke the lines together:

"O Holy Mother of All, we ask that You bless us and hear our prayer.

"Hate is in our hearts: hate for those who have wronged us, and the lust for revenge.

"Touch us now, and take away our hate.

"Touch us now, and help us to forgive.

"Touch us and teach us love for all people, and for all living things.

"As Your children, we ask this favor.

"So mote it be."

"There." Suzanne rose and sat back on the bed with me. "And I will say that prayer also, every night, for so long as it takes me to learn the Law of Love. And to learn what it is that I must do."

"I'm not used to praying at night; I haven't said bedtime prayers since I was seven or eight. But I'll try to remember to do it too. It certainly can't hurt!"

"No. And it may help us very much, indeed! ...Do

you want to look at these sheets any more tonight? Or do we have time now to hypnotize me again?"

"I'll want to memorize the Circle formulas later on, but I guess there's plenty of time between now and..." I checked the sheet listing the Sabbaths... "Lammas."

"You also need to learn the Sabbaths, Jack: that calendar wheel of the witches. Or perhaps you will come to Lammas prepared to dance around a Maypole!"

"I guess I'll need to borrow the sheets sometime, then. Or spend a lot more time over here."

"You would be welcome, I am sure. But the couch is not a very good bed. Especially for someone who sleeps in his underwear. And is ashamed to show that he has skin like everyone else!"

"You love to rub that in, don't you?"

"Rub it...in? Like suntan lotion?"

"I'm sorry. That's a slang expression. It means teasing me about grabbing for that blanket."

"Ah! I understand. Yes, I thought that it was funny, and I still do. But you redeemed yourself: you stalled at the quarry, but you finally did take your clothes off. And after a little while, it did not seem to bother you very much."

"It helped to know I wasn't the only one."

"Yes. And it helped me also, that it took you so long. For otherwise I would have been more ashamed, myself, to show anyone how fat I am. Instead, I could laugh a little at your being ashamed, and forget about my own. Was that a terrible thing to do?"

"No, not really. I guess if we see our own weaknesses in other people, it helps remind us nobody's perfect. Ourselves, least of all! And laughing at things we know are in us too, helps us overcome them.

"You aren't planning to wear your swimsuit tomorrow, are you?"

"No. I will not even take it. Perhaps someday, after I have lost weight, I will remake it into something more comfortable. But so long as the quarry remains private, why should I take the trouble?"

"If you're comfortable without it, you shouldn't. Just don't get burned again."

"You need not fear. That is why I will take the 'large, economy' size of suntan lotion, and probably leave it there. So we will never be without it, just when we need it most!"

"Fine. And I won't need to let Hadrian hypnotize me again, to help me sleep. ...Sue, I think I might have made a big mistake Wednesday night."

"Oh? What mistake?"

"That book I had on telepathy. I put it on my shelf in the room, tucked between two bigger books where I didn't think it would show. But when I came in last night, Hadrian was reading it. Worse yet, I had to agree to let him finish it: that, or let him know about Nick and the rest of us."

"Perhaps it will tell him nothing that he does not already know. Or perhaps he will not believe it when he reads it."

"I wouldn't care to bet on either of those. And he's got a new project: something I'm afraid I gave him the idea for. He wants to get a group together, to study telepathy and hypnosis together scientifically. He says it's never been done before."

"Do you think that anyone will come?"

"He's already put up a notice in the Post Office. Dozens of people might show up. And I'm afraid he'll take advantage of them somehow…unless we do something about it."

"Then we will simply have to join his group: both of us, and perhaps Nick and Alaine as well. Then if one of us must be hypnotized, at least the others will be there. When does he plan to have the first meeting?"

"A week from Monday, in our room in the dorm. If there are too many people, though, we'll probably move it down to that study lounge in E-section."

"You will be there, of course?"

"Unless I have to work late for Doctor Knight, or we spend the evening here."

"No. We should both be there: to protect your room

from the rampaging hordes, and to protect the hordes from Hadrian. Do you think that he will want to hypnotize you, at the meeting?"

"Well, he knows I'm susceptible. At least when I'm tired and I hurt."

"But now you are well, and well-rested. He could not hypnotize you against your will."

"That's true according to Blythe. Sybil Leek doesn't agree, though."

"Then could someone be guarded against one kind of hypnosis, by the use of another?"

"What do you mean?"

"Perhaps I will volunteer to be the subject, instead. You made it easy for me to go back to the Gold Mist. Could you do the opposite?"

"Make you **harder** to hypnotize?"

"Yes: by anyone who does not know the secret, the password. Let me go easily to an early stage: relaxed, but still conscious of what is happening around me. But make me stop there, regardless of what other things Hadrian may try: so that he could never make of me a slave or a toy."

"I guess we could do that. But leave the 'Gold Mist' password to reach the deeper levels?"

She nodded.

"Do you want to do it now?"

"Yes. But first, would you do for me a favor?"

"Sure. What?"

"At the quarry, you rubbed my shoulders and it helped me to relax." She turned away from me. "Would you do it again now? But very gently: remembering that I am still sunburned, just a little?"

"Sure. But with the blouse on this time?"

"Would that not be best? In case Charlie walks in?"

"Yeah." And sliding closer, I started to work. The muscles were knotted, but as I rubbed them through the cloth I felt the knots begin to loosen.

All too soon, though, she pulled away. "Thank you, Jack; that is enough. And now, I think, I am ready." She rearranged the pillows and lay down.

"Relax, then. Relax your body all over. Take a deep breath, and let it out slowly. And now say three times: 'Gold Mist'."

"Gold Mist. Gold Mist. Gold Mist..." Her third repetition was soft and dreamy, and for a long moment afterward she lay silent. Then: "Jack, it **works!** I am standing once more on the stairs, and I can see it all clearly." Her eyes moved from side to side under the lids.

"Good! Now, go on down..."

"You must count with me, from ten down to zero."

"I'm sorry; I forgot. Ten...nine...eight... Zero. Are you at the bottom now?"

"Yes. And the mirror is here where I left it, and my

dress is still hanging on it. And I can see myself...."
She smiled. "I still am not wearing any clothes. And,
Jack: in this place, I am still as thin as before! Will it
always be so?"

"It should, as long as you stick to your diet."

"That is reasonable to me. And it will be one more
reason not to forget!"

"Good. Now, let's see what we can do about
keeping you safe from Hadrian.

"You've already got two layers of protection, I
guess. You need to say 'Gold Mist' yourself, and then
you need me to count you down the steps. But those
are like two doors blocking the same corridor in a big
building. There are probably a lot of other ways to get
where you are, or at least to the same level of hypnosis.
So we need to block all the other corridors, too.

"I'd like you to walk across the floor, and sit down.
Pick the most comfortable-looking chair you see. And
describe it to me."

"It does not look 'comfortable' at all. There are no
arms: only the hard wooden back carved with leaves
and flowers, and a seat covered in dark leather. All
very square and simple." She paused for a moment.
"Well, perhaps it is not quite so bad as it looked...."

"Then settle in. Get as comfortable as you can. And
as you do, close your eyes, and feel yourself growing
even more relaxed than before...more relaxed and

calm than ever before…"

As if settling into some unseen chair, she stirred slightly on the bed and smiled.

"And from now on, whenever you sit in this chair, you'll immediately feel yourself growing just this relaxed. You'll still be mentally alert, but your body will be relaxed, and your mind will be calm: more relaxed and calm than you can ever remember being in your life.

"When you get up, you'll still be that calm and relaxed…and you'll stay that way until you climb the stairs again and come back to Calhoun, or the world it's in. Do you understand?"

"Yes. Jack, I feel wonderful!"

"Great! And now, we'll make sure Hadrian can't pull any dirty tricks on you.

"You'll always be able to come to this place immediately, just by saying 'Gold Mist' three times: just the way you did tonight. But if anybody else is trying to hypnotize you – anybody but Nick or Alaine or me – then you can go down any stairs he wants you to, but they'll be somewhere else in your imagination. So this place will be your very own. And whatever we do here, can't be undone unless that's done here too.

"And no matter what any hypnotist does – myself included! – you'll still be in command of yourself. You won't do anything that's against your moral principles,

or anything you've sworn in a Circle not to do. And if
anybody tries to force you to – even me, or Nick or
Alaine – you'll snap right out of it: right back to normal
reality.

"Do you understand?"

"Yes."

"Can you think of anything I've left out?"

"No."

"Good. Then, I guess we're finished for this
session…"

"No, we are not. If I am to try to read minds for
Hadrian, I would like to try it here: here, where I can
be far more relaxed than ever I will be with him.
Because if I cannot do it here, I will not be able to do
it at the meeting, either. And there is really no purpose
in my volunteering."

"Sure, there is. Even negative evidence is still
evidence…"

"Does that mean that I would be helping to show
hypnosis has no effect?"

"It could help Hadrian decide that, anyway."

"Then let it be as it will be; I will volunteer anyway.
But could we try a test now?"

"I don't have any Zener cards."

"I have never seen them, anyway. Could you not use
ordinary playing cards?"

"Hadrian said there's some technical reason the

Zeners are better. I didn't quite understand it. But he's working on a way to use regular ones instead. Maybe letting us guess the four suits or something."

"If I had a deck of cards, that would be good. But I do not." She was silent for a minute. "But I bought a package of pencils last week, and have not opened it. They are red, and yellow, and green, and blue: six of each, I think. Could you mix them, and take one at a time at random, and have me guess the color?"

"I guess so. Where are they?"

"In the top drawer of the dresser. Probably toward the left side."

The drawer held folded clothes, mostly yellow or blue, but a few school supplies and toilet articles lay on top. Taking out the pencils, I sat back down and opened the package.

"I'm going to close my eyes and pick one. Then I'll open them, and concentrate on the pencil. See if you can guess the color. And I'll write down the colors, and your guesses." I shuffled them from hand to hand, then took one. It was blue. "Ready?"

"I think…yes. It is green."

"Should I tell you if you're right or wrong?"

"No; not until after. Are you ready with another?"

"Not yet." I scribbled "B – G," shuffled the blue one back into the bunch, and with eyes closed, took another: yellow. "Okay: ready."

"Is it…red?"

"You said not to tell you."

"Very well. And the next?"

"…And now, you may tell me. Of the twelve, how many did I guess?"

"By chance, you should have gotten three. But you guessed… two."

"Only two. Then perhaps it is not true. Perhaps hypnosis does not help with telepathy."

"Or maybe we're just not trying the right way. Or one of us is too tired; it's been a long week. Why don't we try again some other time?"

"All right. And now, I think that I am ready to come back up the stairs. For tonight, there are no dirty dishes to wash!"

"…And when I say 'ten', open your eyes and you'll be back in the ordinary world. Feeling fine, alert, not sleepy, and remembering every detail of what we've done.

"One…two… Ten."

She stretched languorously. "Jack, that was very strange. I felt so sure of some of the colors! But still, I guessed only two?"

"I'm afraid so."

"Let me see the paper you used to list them." I passed her the notebook. "…No, you are right. Then perhaps it is all in vain…"

"Maybe we'll be able to convince Hadrian of that. And maybe he'll decide it's not worth running any more tests."

"Perhaps. Or, perhaps he will find someone who will do better. But I am relieved that it will not be me!"

18 Lead Soldiers

May 28-29, 1971

The road was yellow even by moonlight. Its bricks looked old, though, uneven and broken, and great swaths of them were missing.

Ahead rose mountains, the ones from Alaine's card of the Moon, the road rising to pass from sight between the distant towers. Clouds raced across the sky, the huge lunar disk now hidden, now flashing out through breaks between them. My feet were sore, my legs weary, as if I'd been walking this road for hours. If this was a dream, like Suzanne's at the quarry, it was certainly a vivid one!

A break in the clouds left the moon wholly clear for a moment, brighter light spilling onto the land around me. In its light I saw buildings everywhere, some domed, some pillared: temples, I thought, of a thousand different faiths. And yellow too, as if the road's missing bricks had been stolen long ago to build them.

Long ages ago! For these temples were ruined too, the detritus of dead religions: roofs and pillars fallen, domes collapsed, walls crumbling.

As I looked around me the light continued brightening, though clouds quickly hid the moon again. I could see my shadow lying on the shattered bricks ahead, flickering and writhing as if cast by firelight.

Cast by firelight behind me? In sudden dread, I turned and looked.

Wrapped in scarlet flame He towered, and the trident He clutched glowed red-hot, fire wreathing its points. His eyes burned white as slices of the Sun. It was Satan, from some old picture I must have seen in Sunday School. Coming to get me!

I turned and ran, but immediately stumbled on a

loose brick and fell. Trying to stand again, I found the ankle I'd twisted could no longer support me: badly sprained, maybe broken. Painfully I raised myself to my knees then, and turned, and looked up at Satan.

Even as I raised my head He was stooping: taloned hand reaching to pluck me from the ancient road, fanged mouth gaping to swallow me whole. But suddenly He paused, and His sun-eyes turned to one side, away from me.

Someone Else was approaching: white-bearded, robed in swirling clouds, crowned with a tall gray thunderhead in which lightning constantly flickered. In one hand He bore a thick, flat rod of iron like a carpenter's rule. His eyes pits of utter blackness, He scowled at me and Satan alike.

Satan and Jehovah squared off across the ruins, iron rule and flaming trident at the ready. I cowered beneath them on the pavement, trembling, waiting in the silence for the clash of Armageddon: waiting for the world to shatter around me in fire and thunder.

But the silence was broken instead by laughter: by a woman's laughter, like silver chimes in the night. And white light from above paled Satan's fire, outshone Jehovah's lightning, as the clouds split and rolled back to either horizon and vanished.

Still and calm She stood where the Moon had been, Her body shining with the same pale light. Her eyes were like cobalt stars, Her long hair dark as midnight. No robe of cloud, no sheath of flames did She wear: only a silver crescent above Her brow, a necklace of beads, and on one thigh a dark band like a garter.

The Goddess smiled at me, then pointed in stern and silent command at the Two standing above me. For a moment They looked up at Her frozen still as statues, like children caught in some act of petty malice. Then both began to shrink, still frozen: Their fire and lightning dimming, Their colors fading, until both at last gleamed dull and gray as lead.

As They dwindled I saw Another behind Them, standing if He had been there all along. Bare as the Lady's, His body shone with a bronzy light of its own. His eyes and horns were golden. The Others seemed only toys now, lead soldiers before His feet. Picking them up gently, One in each hand, The Horned God straightened.

With the clouds now gone I could see a gigantic wall beyond the mountains, circling this plain of ruins. Past the road's end, past mountains and towers, past even the Goddess, a vast half-seen arch framed darkness.

In a single stride, the Horned One crossed the plain. As His light revealed it more clearly I could see the wall was lined with shelves, all crowded with leaden figures: some in human form, some in the shapes of animals real or fantastic. There must have been thousands of them.

Carefully He placed Satan and Jehovah side by side among the other images. Turning, then, He smiled at me and winked one golden eye.

Stretching out Her hand the Goddess bent and passed it once, moon-gleaming, over me where I lay. At once my pain was gone, my ankle healed, and I rose to face Her. She smiled at me as a mother smiles at a beloved child. Then, turning, She put out a hand to the arch and drew aside the blackness like a curtain...

"...And then They went away into what I guess was Heaven, or maybe the Land of Youth. I couldn't see it; there was just deep green-golden light shining out, so beautiful I almost cried when the curtain closed again. But They left Jehovah and Satan outside on the shelf, in the dark.

"And then, I guess, I woke up. At least, that's all I remember."

"Wow, Jack. That was quite a dream!"

The sun was bright and hot now, beating down into the old quarry. Suzanne and I, wary of sunburn, were thickly smeared with the lotion she'd brought. I'd rubbed it on her back and shoulders, and she on mine. "...But I will spread it on my **front,** myself! And you can spread it on yours."

Even with that protection, though, we'd spent most

of our time in the shade. Nick and Alaine, less vulnerable than we, had lain out in the sun for a while. As the heat had increased, though, even they had retreated to join us.

"So what do you think it means?"

Alaine pondered. "Aunt Theda used to say any dream you remembered that vividly after you woke up held a message of some kind: either from the Gods, or from the deep levels of your own mind. She called them 'postcard' dreams. The picture on the front gets your attention. But if you want the message, you'd better turn it over and read what's on the back!

"And this is a 'postcard' dream if I ever heard one."

"Okay. So what does it say? Can you read it for me?"

She nodded. "I think so. The first part is easy. You've dreamed about the Moon Path before. Last night you saw it again."

"Yeah. But last night it was old and torn up, with a lot of bricks missing."

"'As if they'd been taken', you said, 'to build those temples.' They had!

"Jack, the Moon Path **is** the Old Religion. Almost every other one the world has ever seen was built from its stolen bricks. And most have collapsed again, from their own weight and poor design.

"Because of the centuries of persecution, though, a

lot of the Old Religion itself has been lost. All we really have left are the basic concepts, and the Law of Love, and a handful of chants and rituals and spells. Even those are mostly reconstructions. So those who walk the Moon Path now have to step carefully from brick to brick. Or make their own to fill the gaps."

"All right. I was walking the Moon Path, and suddenly Satan was coming to get me."

"And so was the God of the Old Testament. The two Enemies from your childhood religion were about to fight for your soul, right then and there. And you thought everything was over.

"But then the God and Goddess appeared, and suddenly you saw what had been true all along. Satan and Jehovah were just lead soldiers: toys, puppets, masks, playing pieces in a game. But the Christians had told you the game was real, and you'd believed it...because nobody had shown you it wasn't!

"In your dream, the game was over for a while. And 'God' and 'the Devil' went back on the shelf, back with all the other 'Gods' and 'Devils' the priests have cooked up over thousands of years. And all that was left was the reality behind them all."

"Then the God and Goddess are real, but Satan and Jehovah aren't?"

"What's real? We can't ever really know the Gods, not as They know Themselves. We need to give Them human shapes: shapes that represent Their characteristics as well as we can understand them, and the polarity between.

"But the Christian 'God' and 'Devil' are terrible shapes for Them. There's no balance, no symmetry. You have two grouchy old men: one with a 'rule' of iron, a set of laws you have to obey or else; the other with a hot pitchfork that represents the 'else.' And they fight. They've been fighting forever. If that were true, the Universe would have been destroyed long ago!

"There is a polarity, of course. Even Christians had to recognize some kind of tension between opposites. Without it, the Universe would have no variety: like an infinite bowl of cosmic mashed potatoes. But it isn't a tension between enemies. That kind only destroys."

"Then what is it? I can't believe it's literally male and female. Not in any biological sense."

"No; that's symbolic...or partly so. You can think of them as positive and negative electricity if you like. Older analogies are sun and moon, or fire and water. But in the Old Religion we call them God and Goddess. And in those images, sometimes They appear to us.

"Did they ever have those shapes in reality? Some say yes: that even They were mortal once, or close to mortal, on Earth or some other world. Others, though, say those are just masks for Their real forms:

something we could never fathom or imagine.

"You saw some other things, though, that I've never mentioned to you or put in the material I copied out. You described the Goddess as gleaming like silver, Her hair dark as night, and the God all in tones of bronze and gold. Those are Their traditional, symbolic metals. And have been, ever since metals were first discovered."

"Well, silver is kind of moon-colored, and gold is brighter, like the sun. The High Priestess on your *Book of Shadows* is silver. And you said the Priestess' crown Aunt Theda left you is silver too, with a crescent moon…"

"Even so, that's just one of three. You saw the Goddess with that same crown, but wearing the Band of Law and the Circle of Rebirth too."

"The what, and the what?"

"The garter and necklace you described. The beads of the necklace alternate dark and light, representing the cycle of life and death, and form a circle to show it never ends. The garter you'll learn about later, after you come into First Degree.

"The Goddess, at least as Aunt Theda's Gypsies visualized Her, wears just those three things: exactly as you saw Her. And the Priestess, as Her representative, wears them too. I have my own garter, and Aunt Theda left me her necklace along with the crown. But I'm sure I've never mentioned either one to you!"

"Then how did they show up in my dream?"

"I think it was more than a dream."

"Then what? Some kind of psychic flash, like you got that night from the Moon card?"

She nodded. "If not, then you tell me!"

"Alaine, I don't know. Could I have learned about the necklace some other way, and the garter? Telepathically, maybe?"

"That's possible: especially since it came to you in a dream. We're all more receptive to outside impressions, ESP or whatever, when we're dreaming. But if you'd gotten it that way, why didn't I dream it too?"

"Maybe you did, and you forgot."

"Forget a dream like that? No. I could accept telepathy, but not that. I remember two dreams from last night – I've trained myself to, and write them down the instant I wake up – but neither was like yours."

"Then if not from you, and not from my own subconscious…from where?"

Alaine smiled and gestured with one thumb: upward.

I pondered. "Not from God – Jehovah, I mean – and not from Satan either. From Somebody Else. From the God and Goddess, directly?"

She nodded. "It happens."

"Then, if that's true – and I can't really think of any other explanation – I guess it's time to retire those lead soldiers to the shelf. Up next to Santa Claus and the Tooth Fairy."

Suzanne took my hand. "Does that mean that you will join us? Be a witch?"

"Well, I'm pretty sure I'm not a Christian anymore. That dream showed me Satan and Jehovah for what They are: toys, lead soldiers, Halloween masks. I guess I'd pretty much known that already.

"So They don't scare me now, and They can keep Their Hell and damnation, thank you very much. Their Heaven, too, full of mindless bliss. I had enough of all that as a kid in Sunday school. Now, I'd rather see where the Moon Path goes.

"The scientist in me still isn't satisfied. I'm not sure yet I believe in ESP, much less in casting spells. But I'll accept all that for now as a working hypothesis, to prove or disprove by experiments. And if Hadrian manages to get his group together those are experiments I'll get to watch, and help with.

"So, yes: Sue, Alaine, Nick…and God and Goddess…yes. I'll walk the Moon Path with you, wherever it leads.

"And with your help… Yes. I'll be a witch."

Dramatis Personae

(in order of appearance; as of May 29, 1971):

People at Calhoun:

Jason T. ("Jack") Peredur: a chemistry student, native to Mount Laurel, New Jersey. Recently arrived at Calhoun University in South Carolina to start work toward a graduate degree in chemistry.

Enjoys reading and rock collecting

David Knight, Ph.D.: a celebrated researcher and professor of organic chemistry at Calhoun University. Jack's mentor and thesis advisor.

Suzanne Marat: a freshman liberal-arts major, recently come to the U.S. from Mortagne, Normandy, France on a student visa. Eldest of seven siblings. Loves cooking and dress design. Expert swimmer. Believes in ghosts.

Charlie Blake: another chemistry professor at Calhoun. A self-described "M.S. in a Ph.D. world."

Nicholas ("Nick") Valentine: a former engineering student at Calhoun; from Belvedere, South Carolina. Currently works in appliance repair and runs a light show, the "Flying Fire," saving to go back to class full-time next year.

Hadrian Marsan: a senior physics major at Calhoun, and amateur hypnotist. Believes in telepathy.

Alaine Lancaster: a junior horticulture major at Calhoun, and initiated witch in an English tradition through her Aunt Theda. Reads the Tarot cards.

Gods and Guardians:

The Horned God: well-known to witches. Among other duties, He guards and oversees the Valley of

The Moon Path

Shadows and judges when souls are fit to move on from it to the Land of Youth.

The Goddess: Mother of Gods and Men. Lover of the Horned God. When properly invoked, She will descend upon a willing Priestess to borrow her flesh, walk among us, share Earthly pleasures and teach Wiccan lore and mysteries.

About the Author

Jack Peredur, a New Jersey native, at age 21 moved to South Carolina to pursue higher education at Calhoun University. There he met and became a close friend of the so-called Ravenwood Thirteen.

Stunned by the loss of the Thirteen in the Ravenwood Disaster, Jack found himself unable to complete his Master's Thesis at Calhoun but began keeping diaries instead as a form of home-grown psychotherapy. Changing careers he then became a licensed handyman and builder: first as an employee of Homefixers based in Seven Oaks, and later as its owner.

Since retiring and selling Homefixers in 2007 Jack has devoted himself to travel, research in fields more abstruse than chemistry, refurbishing the old farmhouse and outbuildings near Belvedere which now form the Ravenstead, building an ever-growing network of friends and colleagues, and using those diaries and other sources to create the Ravenwood Series, of which this book is a part.

Jack currently lives at the Ravenstead with his wife, the former Suzanne Marat of Mortagne, France, creator of the Midnight Confections line of intimate apparel; a close-knit group of human friends; and a varying cast of rescued dogs, cats and other "critters."

Jack can be reached by e-mail through the contact page at www.Ravenwood.Associates.

Jack Peredur

72015469R00195

Made in the USA
Columbia, SC
29 August 2019